"What would it take to get you to the altar?"

"If you must know…marriage really isn't on my agenda," Mackie replied.

"Not concerned about your biological clock?"

"I can't believe we're having this conversation. I like my life. It's nice to sleep through the night without being awakened to tend to someone else's needs."

"But what about a lover awakening you to cuddle?"

"I thought we were talking about children."

"You were the one bringing up sleeping undisturbed. Sounds like someone used to sleeping alone."

"Who I sleep with is—"

"Out! Out!" Ashley shrieked. The baby's rebellion against the car seat didn't abate until they arrived back at Mackie's.

Worn from her tantrum, Ashley settled into her makeshift crib, stuck her thumb in her mouth and fell sound asleep. Mackie stared down at the little girl, thinking how enchanting she looked in sleep, how lovable. For the first time in ages, Mackie fantasized about having a baby of her own, then quickly shook her head, drowning such craziness.

The Daddy Dilemma
Kate Denton

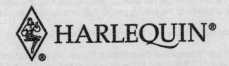

HARLEQUIN®

TORONTO • NEW YORK • LONDON
AMSTERDAM • PARIS • SYDNEY • HAMBURG
STOCKHOLM • ATHENS • TOKYO • MILAN • MADRID
PRAGUE • WARSAW • BUDAPEST • AUCKLAND

ISBN 0-373-03566-7

THE DADDY DILEMMA

First North American Publication 1999.

Look us up on-line at: http://www.romance.net

Printed in U.S.A.

PROLOGUE

THE more Mackie Smith heard, the madder she got. Gordon Galloway was a bully, no...a monster. Mackie pulled a tissue box from her credenza and set it within reach of the sobbing woman seated in front of her desk.

"It's been so long since Ashley was in my arms, so long since my baby—" Beth dissolved into tears again. "I've begged, pleaded for three months...and he refuses even to let me see her."

Attempting to curb her anger, Mackie took a deep breath. Who did Galloway think he was anyway?— riding roughshod over a vulnerable woman...keeping her from her daughter like this. Mackie could hardly wait to move into the courtroom arena and give him a dose of his own medicine. "We're going to do whatever it takes to fix that," she said to Beth. "I promise."

"You don't know Gordon. He'll pull out all the stops. Tell lies...paint me as worse than I was. I realize I made a humongous blunder, but how long do I have to pay for it?"

"Let Mr. Galloway carry on till he's blue in the face," Mackie said. "Fortunately for us, it's the judge who counts and Judge Fillmore won't be swayed by one man's ranting and raving."

"But Gordon can be so convincing." Beth shook her head helplessly. "And he's rich now, too. Rich enough to influence a judge."

Mackie got up from her chair and walked around to pat Beth on the shoulder. "So your former husband has more money than a Swiss bank—that won't sway Fillmore, either." Mackie gave the shoulder a friendly squeeze. "Try to relax and leave the fretting to me. If things go like I hope they will, you'll have your baby in your arms for the weekend."

"A weekend? I want more than that."

"Of course you do. Only our chances are better if we approach this one step at a time. Remember what I told you—first we go for visitation, then we make the pitch for custody down the road."

"But—"

"Beth…" Mackie took her client's hands. "If I'm to be your lawyer, you have to trust me to know what I'm doing."

Beth nodded resignedly.

"Now you'd better get going," Mackie told her. "I'll see you tomorrow at the courthouse…nine sharp." She ushered Beth out of her office.

An hour later Mackie had another file on her desk to draw her attention, but her mind kept returning to the Galloway case. Tucking the ends of her neat brown bob behind her ears, she stared out the window at the montage of Dallas skyscrapers, silently praying that her skills would be enough, that she wouldn't let Beth down. She knew how important her own lawyer's support had been when she was groping her way out of a disastrous marriage. It was equally important to her now to do the same for others. *Would I have left if there'd been a child?* Her breath caught in her throat. Such thoughts were off-limits.

In the predawn hours, Gordon Galloway sat motionless in a rocking chair, watching his tiny daughter sleep. He'd been there the entire night, dozing occasionally, but unable to remain asleep for long. "I can't lose you," he whispered, his heart aching, squeezed in an invisible vise. Yet the possibility was too real. All because of Beth and her hotshot lawyer Mackie Smith.

Already those two were making his life a living hell, and things were just heating up. Gordon could visualize this morning's hearing. Beth had a penchant for drama and the wronged maiden was one of her favorite roles. His imagination went into overdrive speculating on what kind of performance she'd give today to impress this particular audience of one—a judge with the power to blast Gordon's world asunder.

His attorneys had told him to stop stewing, swore that there was no way Beth could finagle Ashley away from him. Easy for them to say—it wasn't their child. And they had yet to catch Beth's act. When she put her mind to it, Beth could charm the fangs off a snake.

For certain, Gordon wasn't about to give up Ashley without a fight—gloves off if necessary, Marquis of Queensberry rules be damned. Yet he couldn't erase the fear that no matter how tough a war he waged, he'd still lose. Even in today's more progressive courts, the norm was to favor mothers over fathers in custody battles. Even mothers like Beth.

He glanced outside. Darkness had given way to a streak of pale pink light traversing the horizon. The dreaded day was here.

Rising stiffly from the chair, his muscles in rebellion at their long confinement, Gordon stretched and crept silently to Ashley's crib, staring down at his daughter. He straightened her blanket, then reluctantly turned away. Time to shower and dress. As apprehensive as he might be about the contest ahead, he dared not be late.

laten in her request. It was already maddening and
an overloaded docket lay ahead of him. The possibility of quickly dispensing with one matter had to be
tempting.

"Counsel," Judge Fillmore said finally, "the other
and

CHAPTER ONE

POISED to present her case, Mackie stood in the center
of the courtroom. Surreptitiously, she glanced at her
adversaries seated at a table a few feet away. Gordon
Galloway and his pack of attorneys from Alexander,
Mott and Percy were awesome to behold. Talk about
overkill. You'd think Galloway was taking on
Microsoft.

"Your Honor," Mackie began, directing her remarks to the judge, "as our petition affirms, my client's ultimate goal is shared custody of her daughter.
However, she wants to be the first to acknowledge
past mistakes and seeks to redeem herself. That's why
I'm submitting a new motion.

"Rather than addressing the custody issue, all we
ask from the court today is that Beth Galloway be
allowed visitations every other weekend for the next
six months, that she be given an opportunity to bond
with her child and to establish herself as a fit
mother."

The stunned silence emanating from the opposing
attorneys told Mackie that reactions were precisely as
she'd anticipated. By admitting weakness and asking
for less than expected, she had robbed the Galloway
team of its chance to beat up on her client.

From Judge Fillmore, Mackie saw a spark of interest in her request. It was already midmorning and an overloaded docket lay ahead of him. The possibility of quickly dispensing with one matter had to be tempting.

"Give me a moment to read the motion," the judge said.

Mackie used the opportunity to study Beth's ex-husband. Earlier she'd spared him scant attention, noting little about his appearance beyond the fact that his medium brown hair was modishly cut. Now she had her chance for a better look.

One wouldn't call him handsome in the conventional sense—his longish face rather angular, no-nonsense wire-rim glasses framing his eyes, his cropped hair ruffled from repeated hand raking. At the same time, something about Galloway made her want to step closer and take stock. Maybe the earnest gaze or the vivid blue eyes that even glasses and distance couldn't hide. There was something understatedly sexy about the man. It was easy to see how an innocent like Beth could have been taken in.

The second the judge laid down Mackie's documents, Sonia Mott, one of Galloway's attorneys, rose to object, only to be cut off in mid-diatribe.

"Have you got some current evidence that shows this mother to be a danger to the child?" the judge interrupted.

"Well..."

"What do you call deserting a newborn?" Gordon Galloway barked in a voice that went all the way to the bench.

"Counselor, control your client," the judge instructed sternly, sending Galloway and his team a stare strong enough to peel paint off the walls. "Petitioner's request is granted. Alternate weekend visitation is temporarily established and further consideration of this matter is postponed for six months. At such time professional assessments will be made." With that, he pounded his gavel, announced a brief recess and left the courtroom.

"We won!" Beth squeezed Mackie's forearms in celebration, then her eyes shot past Mackie's, her lips easing into a sly grin as she zeroed in on her former husband.

Mackie could appreciate her client wanting to gloat a little. But it wasn't wise to toss gasoline on an already-combustible situation. She nudged Beth toward the door. "Get on to that job of yours and I'll negotiate the logistics for Ashley."

After listening stonily to arrangements for relinquishing his child the coming weekend, Gordon walked out with his lawyers as far as the elevators, then pointed at the water fountain, indicating they were to continue on without him. He took a couple of gulps to wash down the bile in his throat. Had his outburst caused the judge to rule in Beth's favor? If it were physically possible, Gordon would kick himself from here to the end of the hall for losing his composure like that.

Normally he displayed the calm, thoughtful demeanor befitting the college professor he was. For a few moments in there, however, he'd been like a child in the throes of the terrible twos—unable to restrain his emotions. But dammit, this was about Ashley. It was torture having her welfare, her future, resting in the hands of others.

I can't leave it like this! Charging back toward the courtroom where Mackie Smith remained behind, Gordon pushed open the door. She was just coming out and he almost collided with her, felt her hand pressing against his chest to avoid bodily contact.

Determined to get himself in control, Gordon retreated a step, bracing himself against one of the courtroom pews. "I tried offering Beth a settlement but she refused," he began, breathlessness from anger and the too-close encounter vibrating in his voice. "Obviously my offer wasn't enough. So please tell me how much she's holding out for and we can move to end this charade."

Mackie was taken aback, not sure what bothered her more—Galloway's reappearance or the physical contact between them. That brief touch was as electrifying as those incredible blue eyes…eyes she could now see were framed by lush sable lashes. Her equilibrium wasn't helped, either, by this revelation about a settlement offer. News to her—Beth hadn't said a word. But that wasn't what mattered at the moment. What mattered was putting some distance between herself and Gordon Galloway. "Really, Mr. Galloway, this isn't appropriate."

He gave her an irritated roll of the eyes. "Neither is your farce of a lawsuit. I repeat, how much?"

"Beth isn't after your money."

''The hell she isn't. Aren't you a tad suspicious that Beth's interest in her daughter comes to life immediately after my inheritance from a rich aunt? Quite a coincidence, wouldn't you agree?''

''Coincidences *do* happen,'' Mackie said, trying to stifle her own irritation. ''And even if everything you're saying is true, the fact remains that we're not supposed to speak without one of your attorneys being present. Goodbye.''

She brushed past him and made for the bank of elevators, stepping inside an empty car. The doors were closing when he reached a hand in and forced them apart, then leaped aboard.

''Our conversation is over, Mr. Galloway.''

''Oh, no, it isn't.''

Mackie didn't respond. She punched at the lobby floor button and glowered malevolently at him.

Gordon could easily read in her scowl what she was thinking. *The man is pure gall.* Well, yes he was—with no apologies. He could be as pushy and obstinate as a salesman on commission when it came to Ashley.

Prissy thing this Mackie Smith was, all puffed up with righteous indignation. If it weren't for that frown and those lips pressed tightly together, she could be quite a knockout. Her figure was stylishly slender, and those green eyes brought emeralds to mind. All in all, though, a bit too flawless for his taste—every hair in place, makeup expertly applied, nails neatly manicured and polished a soft pink. A Neiman-Marcus mannequin come to life. That, or a well-dressed robot.

Galloway, are you crazy? The woman is your enemy. Under the circumstances, her looks rank a zero in importance. Focus man. "Beth's conniving and materialistic," he declared, back on track with Mackie. "She's pretending to want custody in the hope I'll pay her off to drop the suit and go away. Turning down my first offer was simply part of her game."

Mackie maintained her silence and rigid posture, making him even madder. If this stance was meant to discourage, then she'd sorely underestimated the level of his determination. Gordon snatched open the elevator's control box and pushed a button. The car lurched to a halt.

Her frown deepened into a full-fledged glare. "What do you think you're doing?"

"Trying to make you see how it is!"

"Again, this isn't appropriate, Mr. Galloway."

"Appropriate be damned. We're not talking Ms. Manners here. This is about a father fighting like all get-out for his daughter."

Mackie reached for the release button, but he held the panel shut, preventing access.

"Mr. Galloway! You're wasting your time with me. I'm not going to argue the merits of this case with you in an elevator. I'll give you just five seconds to get us moving again before I start screaming my lungs out for a guard."

"OK, OK," he said, throwing up his hands. "I should have known you were too stubborn to reason with. I was hoping to save myself a heap of frustration and spare you some embarrassment. But if you want to play the fool, fine.'' He ran a hand across the back of his neck.

Mackie opened her mouth to yell just as Galloway released the emergency stop button. "Save your vocal cords, lady. You'll need them for court when you start attempting to defend the indefensible. You may have prevailed in round one, but the battle is just starting. And," he added, "be aware that I'll do whatever it takes to hang on to my child."

"That sounds like a threat."

"No, just a friendly warning."

At that moment the doors opened on the ground floor and Galloway stormed off the elevator, leaving Mackie to gape after him. *Friendly?* If that was a friendly warning, she'd hate to be on the receiving end of an unfriendly one.

This guy was unbelievable—a real loose cannon. Sounding off to the judge, waylaying her in the courtroom, holding her captive in an elevator…speaking of which… People getting on made Mackie aware she'd better exit unless she planned to spend the day riding up and down. She walked to her car in the parking lot, still fixated on Galloway.

Loose cannon or not, he seemed so sure of his position, so adamant that Beth was not what she made herself out to be. Could he even be half right? Could money possibly be on Beth's agenda? If so, why had Beth never so much as hinted that she sought part of her ex-husband's recent financial windfall? If it was important, why hadn't she revealed that she'd already been offered a share?

No, Galloway was simply shooting off his mouth, talking when he should have kept silent. What Mackie had just witnessed was the bruised pride of a wounded Texas male. His ego, battered by the desertion of his wife, had overridden his ability to think clearly and created a need to strike back. She must concentrate on that and not let him undermine her relationship with her client.

After all, Beth hadn't tried to sugarcoat her role in her predicament. She claimed her actions had been triggered by postpartum depression, yet she hadn't let herself off the hook. From day one, she'd owned up to irresponsible behavior. But simply because she'd misbehaved—even grievously—in those early weeks of motherhood was no excuse for Gordon Galloway's punishing her by forever withholding her child. Beth had a right to be with her daughter and Ashley had a right to know her mother. As for Galloway's rights— well, let Alexander, Mott, et cetera worry about them. Mackie had her own problems.

"What if he doesn't bring her?" It was five minutes until six on Friday and Beth was planted in front of the window of the conference room adjacent to Mackie's office, monitoring the parking lot for incoming cars.

"He will." Mackie spoke more with bravado than conviction. During the proceedings and afterward, Galloway had acted mad enough to take the law into his own hands and defy a court order. Or to keep the opposition waiting till the last minute simply for the devilment of it. She glanced at her watch. Five fifty-nine now.

A knock sounded at exactly six. He must have been parked on the street. "You're here," Mackie said, her throat catching at the sight of the picture before her—Galloway carrying a precious little girl.

"Regrettably," he said solemnly, his attitude bringing her back to earth.

She opened the door wider and gestured toward the conference room, studying the two as she followed behind.

The toddler was dressed in a pink coat trimmed with fake fur. Beneath the matching pink hat curled soft brown ringlets. Her blue eyes, exact copies of her father's, took in Mackie from her shoulder-high view.

Beth stood transfixed at the back of the room as Gordon shifted a diaper bag off his shoulder onto the conference table. Neither spoke to the other.

Mackie walked over and urged Beth forward. "Come greet your daughter."

Seemingly afraid to get too close to Gordon or Ashley, Beth tentatively approached. She reached out to take the baby from Gordon.

As if programmed by her father, Ashley let out a howl the instant Beth touched her. But instead of turning into the familiar male shoulder, the little girl flung herself toward Mackie's arms. Mackie, nonplussed, gingerly took Ashley and held her as one might cradle a large cactus plant. "There, there," she said uncomfortably, aware of Galloway's scrutiny as she tried shifting the bundle to her hip.

"Lord help me," he growled. "Give her back before you drop her. You're as bad as your client—" he cast a menacing glance at Beth "—neither one with the maternal instincts of a cuckoo bird."

For a moment Mackie reeled from the tongue-lashing, but then managed to regain her poise. "Insults won't make this any easier, Mr. Galloway," she huffed, again shifting the load in her arms and leaning her head out of reach of the curious little fingers trying to snag a gold earring.

"OK, I'll keep quiet. Just give her to me."

Mackie refused to relinquish the baby to him, defiantly handing her to Beth instead. Ashley's lips curved down at the exchange but at least she didn't start wailing again. Turning back to Galloway, Mackie announced crisply, "We won't keep you any longer. This transaction is complete."

"Transaction?" Galloway's face darkened ominously. "Is that how you see it—a transaction?" He gave a puff of disgust. "Man. You and Beth are definitely kindred spirits."

"And you're a sore loser. What say we give the put-downs a rest and you be on your way? Beth has waited a long time for this reunion with her daughter. Why don't we let them get to it?"

"Right...a long time," he said, sparing no sarcasm. Then his shoulders seemed to sag a little in defeat. "I'll be available all weekend if you need me, Beth. I've brought some clothes and toys, and a list of things she likes and dislikes. I'll leave her car seat with the guard downstairs…oh, and here…''

Placing two business cards on the table, he slid one Beth's way and one toward Mackie. ''My home and cell phone numbers are on the back. I expect to be notified immediately if there's the slightest problem.''

''There won't be,'' Mackie answered optimistically, motioning Gordon toward the door. He put a hand up to wave to his daughter, then departed.

''Well, thank heavens that's over,'' she said, smiling to Beth once he was gone. The smile faded immediately as Mackie moved her gaze to Ashley whom Beth had set on the conference table. In that brief period of time the child had upended a silver carafe, which was sending rivulets of water toward the business cards. Beth seemed oblivious to the spill.

''Better get those cards,'' Mackie admonished. ''While they're still readable.'' All hell would break loose if something happened to Ashley and Galloway weren't informed.

Compliantly Beth reached for Ashley and the cards.

''Now let's get you down to the car so you can spend the next two days getting acquainted.'' Mackie started gathering up the paraphernalia. ''You're in charge now,'' she said, turning to Beth.

Beth, who should have been euphoric, wore a dazed expression. ''I can't believe it's happened. I expected something else to go wrong at the last minute, to…to…''

''Everything's gone exactly as intended, so you can rest easy.''

Beth cleared her throat. "Not exactly everything."

"Is there a problem?" Mackie asked. "Something you haven't told me? I'm aware of Gordon's settlement offer. Is it that?"

Beth's eyes seemed to become shuttered. "No, not that." She slid into a chair, Ashley on her lap. "I'm almost afraid to tell you."

Mackie patted her arm comfortingly. "Don't be silly—there's nothing you can't share with me. And whatever it is, we can handle it." Mackie held her breath. Despite her encouraging words, she had a feeling she didn't want to hear this.

"I was hoping you'd say that, but I'm in your debt so much already. I owe you big time, Mackie. Your support, your—"

Mackie signaled whoa. "We can't start handling it until I know what's wrong."

"I need you to watch Ashley for me."

"What!"

"I have to go back to the restaurant. You know I'm not supposed to work weekends...but there's a big party scheduled...then Tammy called in sick...so there's no one to act as hostess, manning the reservations desk, greeting people and seeing them to their tables. Rick told me I *have* to be there. If not, he'll fire me. It's just for a few hours. I'll be off by ten or ten-thirty. But I can't lose this job."

Mackie panicked. *Just a few hours?*—might as well be a few years. She knew next to nothing about babies. Why, up until ten minutes ago, she'd never even held one. She wasn't antikids—they just weren't part of her life. Years ago she'd decided on career over motherhood.

"I don't do children," she said to Beth. "Why didn't you tell me earlier so we could have postponed—"

"Postponed?" Beth's voice took on a strident note. "Gordon would have loved that, now wouldn't he? Just prove everything he's been saying about me is true. You know I don't have anyone else—no girlfriends, no family here—so please, please, please, can you look after Ashley this evening?" Beth reached out and grasped Mackie's hand.

Mackie sighed. She'd promised to go the distance with Beth. What could she do but agree?

Ashley was cute to look at, but about as easy to control as a young chimpanzee. From the second Mackie had arrived at her town house with the toddler in tow, the latter had been expressing her displeasure with the arrangement. She'd turned up her nose at dinner, rebelled at having her diaper changed and refused to stay in the playpen Mackie had borrowed from a neighbor, preferring to roam around the unfamiliar territory.

Pricey art books, marble fruit and crystal obelisks now cluttered the mantel, secure from Ashley's reach. Although by now Mackie would willingly sacrifice any one of them to Ashley's mayhem if that would keep the baby from sobbing and pitifully begging for her "Da Da" the way she was doing.

"Don't cry. Please stop crying." Mackie cast her eyes upward in supplication. *Where are you, Beth?*

Pacing the floor with the fussy baby in her arms, Mackie noticed the warmth of her skin. She leaned her head back for a better view of the child's face. It was flushed and tearstained. "Is it too hot in here? Or do you have a fever?" *Don't you dare have a fever.*

At eleven-thirty, every shred of patience and energy exhausted, Mackie called the restaurant. "Beth Galloway, please."

"Sorry, ma'am. Beth's gone."

Mackie hung up the phone. *Hallelujah! Beth's on her way.*

For thirty more minutes Mackie circled the room and watched the time crawl by. Where was Beth? What could she possibly be doing? An accident perhaps. Or maybe she'd forgotten and gone home. She dialed Beth's apartment. No answer. Of course Beth hadn't forgotten—something was definitely wrong.

The waiting was getting intolerable. Ashley crying...Mackie worrying now about both Ashley *and* Beth.

Finally deciding she could no longer put off the inevitable, Mackie placed a weepy Ashley in the playpen with a bottle of milk to distract her, then fished out Gordon Galloway's card from her briefcase and dialed his number.

"Mr. Galloway, this is Mackie Smith, Beth's attorney. I know it's late, but—"

"Has something happened to Ashley?"

"I don't think it's anything serious but she may be running a fever. If you'll give me directions to your home, I'll bring her there right away."

"Did you take her temperature?"

"Uh, no. Not yet."

"Did you even think about it?"

"No, frankly I didn't. I've been too busy walking the floor with her the last four hours."

"Give me the address. It'll be quicker for me to come there."

Mackie rattled off her street name and number.

"I'll be there in fifteen minutes." He hung up before Mackie had a chance to say another word.

When the phone rang seconds later, Mackie guessed it was Galloway asking for directions. But it was Beth.

"Mackie, it's me."

"Beth, where are you? I've been frantic."

"I'm fine...it's a long story."

Mackie, frazzled and not mollified by Beth's non-answer, snapped, "Then give me the condensed version."

"Uh-oh, I was afraid you'd be upset."

"Upset? You might say that. First you spring the news you have to work, then you don't come when you say you will—"

"My car stalled on the freeway, Mackie. I've been stranded for over an hour praying for someone to stop and help. A policeman's here now and we're waiting for a tow truck."

"Jeez...that's scary." The thought of what *could*

have happened when Beth's clunker of a car gave out sent a chill through Mackie.

"Tell me about it," Beth groaned. "But *you all* are OK, aren't you?"

"Ashley's restless. I think she may be running a fever."

"Probably just a minor thing," Beth replied. "Listen, I don't know how long this will take and it's late already. I think it'd be best for you to keep Ashley until morning. Oh, the wrecker's here, gotta go."

"Don't hang up!" But the plea was too late. For the second time in less than ten minutes, Mackie heard only a dial tone at the end of a telephone line.

Gordon had grabbed his keys from the kitchen counter and raced out to the garage within seconds of ringing off from Mackie Smith. He hoped he could drive, unnerved as he was by this turn of events. He'd wanted Ashley back, but not this way. What was going on with his baby? He had heard her whimpers in the background.

At least luck was partially on his side. It was late, but he was still dressed, so he hadn't been delayed throwing on clothes. And Mackie's place wasn't that far away.

Mackie opened the front door of her town house just as Gordon's finger started to hit the bell. "Where's Ashley?" he demanded, rushing inside.

"*Shh.*" Mackie put a finger to her lips. Together she and Gordon tiptoed toward the middle of her living room where Ashley lay in the playpen, rump in the air, thumb in her mouth, sound asleep. "She's fine now."

Gordon bent over, gently placing the back of his hand on Ashley's forehead. Her brow was cool. He straightened up. "No fever and her coloring's good. Probably just upset over having her life upended." A flinty glare punctuated the gibe to ensure that it wouldn't escape Mackie's notice.

Reassured that Ashley was indeed fine, Gordon looked around. Something was wrong with this picture. "Where in Hades is Beth? Why's Ashley here with you?" He'd been too scared before to question why Mackie Smith was the one who had called him. Now he wanted some answers.

"Uh…there was an unavoidable emergency."

"…'an unavoidable emergency,'" he repeated. "Right…I'll just bet." A pause, then a derisive chuckle. "You'll find Beth's whole life is a series of 'unavoidable emergencies.' Another one of those endearing foibles of hers I tried to tell you about. Beth's a manipulator, using everything and everybody to get what she wants. Believe me, I could cite chapter and verse—"

Mackie gave an impatient sigh. "I'm sure you're relishing this opportunity to throw in a few more slurs about Beth, but it's been a long day and I'm too tired to spar with you right now."

Gordon heard the weariness in her voice and almost felt sorry for her. This was not the poised, self-confident woman he'd dealt with earlier. A few hours ago she'd been bandbox perfect—tailored wool suit, shiny gold earrings, spotless black pumps. Then, he'd come close to hating her—and her ability to tear his and his daughter's life into shreds without breaking a sweat. This woman looked exhausted and vulnerable. Stained silk blouse hanging loose over her skirt, one earring missing, shoes off and a gaping run snaking up a leg of her sheer stockings. Quite a contrast.

She became aware of his assessment, smoothing back her mussed hair and tucking in her blouse. "Well..." she began, "guess it was only a false alarm. Go back home. We'll be OK."

Gordon cocked an eyebrow. "I don't think so."

"You saw for yourself, Ashley isn't sick. Sorry I bothered you, but there's no point in your hanging around."

"I won't be 'hanging around.' I'm taking my daughter home."

"I can't let you do that."

"Try and stop me."

"You know full well I can't, but the judge's order can."

"Nice try, Ms. Smith. Only the order says Ashley's *mother* has visitation privileges this weekend. It says nothing about some hired hand laying claim to her. Besides, an hour ago you were ready to bring her to me."

"Things have changed since then." Mackie's brain raced. "Surely you know the position you're placing me in."

"You'll forgive me if I don't get overly concerned with your 'position.'"

"OK then, think about yourself. From where I'm sitting, Judge Fillmore isn't all that fond of you. He isn't keen on being sassed in court. Whether or not Beth violated the terms of her visitation—and that remains to be seen—if you take Ashley, then you will be too. Do you want to chance riling the judge even more, and possibly strengthening Beth's hand when we do pursue joint custody?"

Gordon seemed to mull that one over. And while he was, Mackie added, "Besides, Ashley is down for the night. Why wake her up when she's already had a bad evening?"

More mulling on Gordon's part. "I'm not about to walk out of here without my daughter. Yet you do have a point about not waking her up." Gordon wasn't about to concede any other points. "I'll just camp out until Beth shows up."

"No way. I must insist—"

"Insist till doomsday. I'm not leaving my daughter in the care of a stranger who clearly doesn't know much about small children. Unless you think you're strong enough to throw me out."

"I wish."

"Then you have a choice—either you get Beth over here pronto or I stay the night."

CHAPTER TWO

GORDON'S pronouncement caused Mackie to throw her hands in the air. "So stay! But just so you know...I own one bed, which I have no intention of giving up. Or sharing. That leaves the couch for you and, as you can see, it's sixty inches at best." She gave a smirking assessment of his six foot plus frame. "I'm sure you'll get lots of sleep."

"Probably more than I was going to get before, worrying about Ashley with Beth. At least I'll be able to ensure Ash is OK."

"Well now that everything's resolved to your satisfaction, I'm going upstairs to change into something more comfort—" Mackie stopped. All she'd meant to convey was that she was getting out of her work clothes, but the words were classic innuendo.

"Into something else," she corrected. "Then I plan to have a sandwich. I haven't eaten since lunch." Without waiting for a response, she started up the stairs. Gordon remained behind in silence, yet with every step, she could feel his eyes following her ascent.

Minutes later, when Mackie returned to her living room dressed in an old pair of gray sweats, Gordon wasn't there. She went to the kitchen and found him hunched over her refrigerator, pulling out packages of deli ham and cheese. Lettuce and a ripe red tomato were already draining on a paper towel by the sink.

"Making yourself right at home I see."

"I haven't eaten much today, either. Hope you don't mind my helping myself. If you do, just bill me."

Mackie rolled her eyes and handed him a loaf of seven-grain bread from the pantry. "Feel free...and while you're at it, you can fix me a sandwich, too. Mustard, no mayonnaise.

"What do you want to drink?" she asked, replacing him at the refrigerator. "Milk? Beer? Water?"

"Whatever you're having."

"I hate that," Mackie said. "Just pick what you prefer." She set a Michelob on the counter along with a half gallon of milk.

"Milk. OK?"

Gordon had finished assembling the sandwiches and placed one in front of her, watching as Mackie poured milk into their glasses. "And what else do you hate?"

"Blue eye shadow, party cocktail wieners drenched in messy barbecue sauce, smokers puffing away at the next table in a restaurant," she answered nonchalantly, carrying her food to the glass-topped table.

"Strange, isn't it," Gordon said, grabbing a napkin and joining her.

"What's strange?"

"Us sitting here eating together like a couple of old friends."

Her expression was one of incredulity. "Oh, I hardly think anyone would mistake us for friends."

"Disgruntled married couple then."

"Bad image, but closer."

"Too close. I'd say we're experts on bad marriages and the fallout that goes with them."

"What do you know about me and my marriage?" Mackie said warily. He was right, but the details of her miserable four years with Bruce weren't common knowledge.

"Nothing. Actually I was referring to your profession, not you personally. However, few people get into their thirties without taking the plunge at least once. Have you had a bad experience?"

A disastrous one. But the scars of her marriage— a bruised heart and pummeled psyche—were none of Galloway's business. "It's no secret I've been married," she admitted, "but it's not a subject I care to talk about."

"Well, if we're going to spend the night together, I think I should know something more about you than your name and marital status, don't you?"

"If we were 'spending the night together,' as you put it, that might be true, but you're only bunking on the couch. There's no need for a round of true confessions."

"Any children?" he persisted.

"As I said, I don't want to talk about my past."

"No, no children," Gordon said. "Silly question anyway. It's obvious your experience with kids is nil.'' He leaned back in his chair. "So...what about brothers, sisters?"

"Mr. Galloway, you're slow to catch on. There's no reason for us to make small talk or to try to get better acquainted."

"No, I suppose there isn't. Besides, I wouldn't want you to accuse me of taking advantage of your hospitality. It's obvious you're tired and sleepy." He took a last bite from his sandwich and drained the glass of milk. "Go on up to bed and I'll rinse the dishes and wrap up the food."

Mackie was past caring whether the dishes got rinsed or the food wrapped. She was fading fast and relieved that Galloway understood that much. Maybe he wasn't willing to leave, but at least he wasn't going to be a demanding guest. "Whatever," she said. "I'm going to bed."

"By the way..." Gordon's voice stopped Mackie just as she reached the door of the kitchen. "Do you happen to have a spare toothbrush?"

Mackie eyed him skeptically as if the question was loaded. Then she said. "Medicine cabinet. Guest bathroom."

Gordon watched her leave and pondered her reaction to him. Mackie Smith was one skittish lady. Was it the attorney or the unhappy divorcée showing through? Mackie was hard to read. She'd reacted to the marriage question and the innocuous family question as if she were a prisoner of war required to give only name, rank and serial number. Then he remembered—this *was* war. She and Beth on one side, he and Ashley on the other. Mackie Smith wasn't forgetting that and neither should he. He shouldn't be letting his guard down or getting too chummy.

Mackie slept until nine the next morning, waking with a start when she realized how late it was. Shrugging quickly into her robe, she tore downstairs, fearful she'd find the Galloways long gone.

Once in the kitchen, her anxiety subsided as she came upon the two having breakfast together. Ashley, sitting on the cabinet, was eating slices of banana. Gordon, standing in front of her, was drinking coffee and coaxing the baby to take spoonfuls of cereal.

"I...uh, I overslept," Mackie said, flustered and searching for something to say. She was glad the chenille robe was strictly of the utilitarian variety. Galloway's peep show was enough. He was dressed, but his shirt was unbuttoned and hanging loose, revealing an expanse of furry chest. Maybe it was because she wasn't used to bare chests in the morning, but the view of male flesh was disconcerting. She averted her gaze. "I need coffee—bad."

"Coffee's made," he said hostlike, gesturing toward the nearly full carafe as if they were in his kitchen rather than hers.

Mackie poured a cupful, holding the mug with both hands as she watched the interaction between the Galloways. "You found something for her to eat."

"Yeah, been rummaging again. I'm grateful you're not the type of woman who stocks only tofu and sprouts."

"A compliment? That's almost too much to handle first thing in the morning."

"Don't worry, I'll make up for it later."

"I'm sure you will."

The baby, tiring of the cereal and the adult conversation, pushed away the spoon in her father's hand and centered her attention on Mackie.

"Hi," Mackie said tentatively.

The little girl didn't answer, but did respond with a grin of tiny teeth.

The grin was irresistible and Mackie could only smile back. "Is she feeling OK this morning?" she asked Gordon.

"She's great."

"That's good." At least there wasn't a pediatric health crisis facing her, Mackie thought. *So what do I do now?* Beth would be arriving before long and it might be dicey if Gordon was still around when she did. Addressing that was priority number one. "Don't mean to rush you along," she said, "but since everything's under control, why don't you run on home? Beth should be here soon."

"You don't get it, do you? For a sharp legal eagle..." He shook his head as if unable to believe anyone capable of such naivete. "First, I'm staying till Beth shows. Second, don't hold your breath waiting for that to happen. God only knows when it'll be. Experience says she'll come when she's good and ready. My money's on tomorrow. About a half hour before her visitation's due to end."

Mackie encountered enough strife in court appearances during the week and wanted only peace and quiet on the weekends. Today that appeared about as likely as Galloway turning into a nice human being. She was mentally composing a nifty retort when the telephone rang.

"Mackie?"

"Good morning, *Beth*." Smugly Mackie cast her eyes at Galloway who was monitoring her conversation. "How's the car thing going?"

Big sigh from Beth. "You know mechanics. I'm sitting here at the garage cooling my heels and now he tells me it's going to be midafternoon before it's fixed. A part has to be sent over. There's no way I can get to your place before three. Go ahead and tell me I'm the worst client ever, but I need to beg for another favor. Can you keep Ashley a bit longer?"

A bit? Three o'clock was almost six hours from now. But what choice did she have? "I suppose I can hold down the fort until three."

"You're a dear, Mackie. I'll be there as soon as I can. Promise."

"Car trouble...that was the emergency? She used to be more original than that," Gordon taunted as Mackie hung up the phone.

"Give it a rest," Mackie snapped. "Beth's doing the best she can. Not everyone can afford cars that don't break down at the most inconvenient times. Shiny new Infiniti vans like you've got parked out front don't fit most budgets."

"Would Beth go away if I bought her a new car? She can have an Infiniti, too, if she wants. Or a

Mercedes. Her choice. You can tell her that if she ever arrives. As for me and Ash, we're going home.''

"Leave with my blessings, only Ashley stays here.''

"No way. When Beth comes, I'll zip right over here and hand Ashley over…just like the judge ordered. But in the meantime, I need a shower and she needs a chance to wander around somewhere safe.''

Mackie bristled. "You act like my home is seeded with land mines.''

"Almost. You're damn sure not equipped for a fifteen-month-old. Those steep stairs are a hazard to grown-ups much less kids and I have yet to spot a plug protector or cabinet guard.

"Besides, how long do you think that white upholstery and those oriental rugs will hold up to a toddler's abuse?''

"That's my problem.''

"No, it's Beth's problem and she's not here to handle it. I don't think the judge gave Ashley's *mother* temporary custody for the weekend only for her to turn around and transfer it to her lawyer.''

"There *are* extenuating circumstances here, Mr. Galloway,'' she protested. "And most *reasonable* people would extend some leeway to Beth. After all, car problems can be overwhelming.''

Gordon took off his glasses and rubbed his eyes. "Be that as it may, if it weren't the car, then Beth would find something else to be overwhelmed about. She always does. She was overwhelmed when she got pregnant, when she delivered, when she came home with the baby. Do you realize that she ignored her daughter from the very beginning? Didn't want to hold her, cuddle her, feed her?''

"Symptoms of postpartum depression at its most severe,'' Mackie defended.

"A lot of women suffer depression after giving birth but they don't abandon a month-old infant like Beth did.''

"How can you blame her for something she had no control over? Her behavior was the result of a medical condition.''

Gordon poured more coffee into his cup, then turned to face her. ''I blame her because I think she latched on to the handy label of postpartum depression to get sympathy. She's got a medical condition all right—she was born without a heart. And there's no cure for that.''

"Why are you so hostile, so unforgiving? You don't give your former wife an inch.''

Gordon, agitated, almost sloshed the coffee out of his cup. ''Lady, my concern is for my daughter. If you were in my shoes, you'd act just like me. Only you're not, and you don't know what you're talking about.''

"I know a lot more than you think.''

"I'm aware you're a family rights advocate, a do-gooder who volunteers a lot of hours to help women who are down and out—''

"Been checking up on me?'' she broke in.

"Through my attorneys. It pays to know a little about your adversaries. The point I'm trying to get to is that with your background, surely you've come across one or two rotten apples who need a boot to the behind more than a pat on the head.''

"Yes, but that's not the case here—"

Before she could speak further, they were interrupted by Ashley's tearing up.

"Look at that. We're upsetting her," Gordon scolded. "She isn't used to hearing adults' squabbling."

"The last thing I want to do is make Ashley cry. But don't expect me to simply remain mum while you attack my client."

"Forever loyal. You're probably..." Gordon shook his head. "You're probably even representing Beth pro bono. That's it, isn't it? You're busting your rear, providing her legal representation, even taking care of her child, and Beth's not even paying you a fee."

Mackie grimaced. From Gordon's lips, her humanitarian deed sounded like the height of stupidity. What was it to him, anyway? "My being paid or not paid is immaterial. I'll have you know—"

In the midst of being read the riot act, Galloway flashed her a disarming smile. "Actually it is material," he said. "Clues me in to the fact that you and I have something in common."

"We do? I can hardly imagine what."

"Being totally taken in by a con artist, that's what. Welcome to the club."

Her eyes flashed. "Don't patronize me. You can take your club and stuff it."

Surprisingly Gordon laughed and in spite of herself, Mackie did, too.

He put his hands on her arms. "How about a compromise?"

She eyed him suspiciously, stepping back. "What kind of compromise?"

"If I leave, you're going to have the same situation as last night—Ashley in a strange place with a strange person. Most likely being pretty vocal about not liking the situation. Since Beth won't be here for hours, come home with me so I can shower and shave and Ashley can have some time in familiar surroundings. Then we'll get back over here by midafternoon. Deal?" He stuck out his hand for a shake.

Mackie thought for a moment, then accepted his offer. His touch was warm, his long fingers wrapping around her own. This was not at all like a business handshake, more of a caress. Uncomfortable, she pulled free, then excused herself. "OK, Mr. Galloway, I'll be ready to leave in a half hour."

"Do you think you could call me Gordon? This Mr. stuff is getting pretty tiresome."

"All right then…Gordon."

The neighborhood was beautiful with its wide curvy streets and stately old homes. The St. Augustine grass favored in Dallas now lay in a dormant strawlike phase, but the live oaks were vigorously holding on to their rich greens and the hearty pansies added a flash of color to the oversize lawns.

Gordon's house was a two-story of brick and

Austin stone showcased nicely by landscaped grounds and imposing trees. It was charming, warm and inviting.

They parked at the curb and Mackie followed Gordon and Ashley up a brick path to the front door. Still balancing Ashley in his arms, Gordon unlocked the door and motioned Mackie inside.

A tortoiseshell cat came padding down the staircase to check out the group. As Mackie shed her jacket and purse and deposited them on a coat tree, the cat circled her ankles. "And who is this?" Mackie reached down to stroke the animal who responded with a loud purr.

"Cleo. She likes you already because you're older than fifteen months and haven't tried to pick her up by the tail. Poor thing is accustomed to being chased, teased and manhandled as only a toddler can do. Half my waking hours are spent protecting her from Ash's clutches."

He escorted Mackie into a large family room, with French doors leading to a patio and pool area. Depositing his daughter on the sofa, he took off her coat and bonnet. "Will you watch Ash while I clean myself up?"

"Sure." Mackie cast a wary glance at the toddler as Gordon left the room. "Go easy on me," she implored the child who had eased off her perch and was busily ripping pages from a magazine.

He stuck his head back in. "Put on a *Barney* video and she'll be putty in your hands."

Grateful for the hint, Mackie did just that. Ashley

got back up beside her on the couch mesmerized by the purple dinosaur on the television. Mackie sat watching Barney for the first time in her life and then, entranced, watched Ashley swaying to the music and clapping her hands enthusiastically.

In a few minutes, Gordon reappeared in jeans and a jacquard-weave sweater, his hair damp from his shower. "Now to get Ash ready," he announced. "Or would you like to be the one to give her a bath?"

"Funny man," Mackie answered. "I'll just wait here for the two of you."

At Gordon's suggestion, they agreed to pass the time till Beth's scheduled appearance tending to weekend errands. First picking up photographs at the camera shop, then a visit to an open-air mall to purchase shoes for Ashley, after that a stop at the pet store to buy cat food for Cleo.

It wasn't yet one o'clock but Mackie was ready for a break. This routine was daunting. She stretched within the confines of her seat belt.

"Bored?" Gordon asked.

"More awed than bored. And maybe a tiny bit fatigued. I do these same sorts of chores every Saturday, but a child definitely adds a…um…a new dimension." She glanced at Ashley in her car seat punching the buttons of a toy mobile telephone, causing a racket of beeps and bells.

"'New dimension.' That's a diplomatic turn of phrase. You mean new dimensions like packing the car safari-style with toys, snacks, diapers, what have you...then buckling her in a car seat, arriving at your destination, unbuckling, getting out strollers, putting back strollers...whew, makes me tired just to think of it.'' He grinned. ''If I didn't love having her with me so much, I'd give in to exhaustion myself.'' Glancing at his watch, he said, ''It's lunchtime. What say we grab a bite somewhere? Preferably a place where we can order something speedy. Ash has a short attention span in restaurants.''

''Sounds good. Do you have a restaurant in mind?''

He thought for a moment. ''There's an Italian place in Highland Park Village where we can dine alfresco. She likes that.''

The day was crisp but not cold, perfect weather for eating outside. After getting a table and a high chair for Ashley, they ordered salads and pizza.

''Who takes care of Ashley while you work?'' Mackie asked.

''A part-time nanny. I have an arrangement with a wonderful lady who comes to the house three days a week. She adores Ashley and vice versa.''

''And the other two work days?''

''I don't have classes then so I take care of her myself.''

''That doesn't leave much time for a social life, or for going out.''

He raised an eyebrow. ''Fishing for some tidbit to use against me? Like my admitting to having a different woman over every night?''

''It was a simple observation,'' Mackie said

grumpily. "Next you'll be accusing me of taping our conversations for evidence."

"Sorry. But it's hard not to be paranoid. You and I do have conflicting interests."

"Believe it or not, I care about Ashley's welfare, too."

"If you did, you'd be fighting for me. For a family rights champion, you're on the wrong side in this one, Mackie. That woman—"

Mackie held up a hand. "—is someone who deserves a second chance. She's really turning her life around—counseling, college courses, a hostess job at Café Maurice, even joined a church—"

"Gee, a regular saint. Probably be selected Dallas Mother of the Year," Gordon sniped.

"Why don't we just focus on our salads instead of on the case?"

Both were silent for a time, then the tension was lifted by Ashley, who began acting like a little coquette. First flirting with the man at the adjoining table, grinning every time he looked her way, then with the waiter whom she cast her eyes at while trying to heist pencils from his apron pocket.

Gordon and Mackie couldn't help but laugh at his daughter's outrageous ways. "I pity the boys when she gets older," Mackie said.

"I pity *me*."

The pizza arrived and they ate and talked, both trying to keep the conversation innocuous. The food was delicious and none of the other diners seemed offended by the mess Ashley was creating. A flock of birds could have feasted on the leavings beneath the child's high chair. Broken saltines, a tomato slice, chunks of pizza crust. A line was crossed, however, when Ashley tossed her cup down and splattered Mackie's shoes with milk.

"That's it—time to go," Gordon said, signaling for a check. "She always starts clearing the table when she's getting restless."

Once they were back in the car, Gordon said, "In answer to your question at the restaurant—after being married to Beth, I've pretty much cooled it on socializing with the opposite sex."

Mackie was surprised, and strangely elated, that he'd bothered to explain. So Gordon Galloway was not only single, but available. She tried to squelch the pleasure she felt at that bit of information, deciding it was safer to keep feuding. "Some people would say you're a cynic."

"And some people would be right. Since news spread of my inheritance, the number of women lining up to be the next Mrs. Galloway is enough to make any man cynical. I never had to beat off women with a stick before."

I find that hard to believe. Money wasn't Gordon Galloway's main draw. Not with that killer grin and those clear blue eyes that called to mind a mountain lake. Mackie caught herself, appalled by her own thoughts. This was totally unacceptable…engaging in such musings about an opponent. An opponent who was the biological equivalent of pond scum according to his ex-wife. "So why beat them off," she persisted. "Don't you think Ashley needs a mother?"

Gordon gave her a chiding, "Tsk, tsk." "And here you've been telling me she already has a mother, a dear loving one, in Beth. Or was your question whether I plan to remarry? Ms. Smith, you're getting very personal. Are you interested?"

Mackie fought back an embarrassed flush. "Don't flatter yourself. I couldn't get interested in you even if I wanted to. Ethically you're a no-no. Besides, I'm not one of those predatory women who favors a man solely because he happens to have a big bank balance."

Gordon chuckled. "So a man's money doesn't appeal. What *would* it take to get you to the altar?"

"I'll pretend you didn't ask that."

"Oh I see, *your* personal questions are acceptable, *mine* aren't."

"OK, if you must know...marriage really isn't on my agenda."

"Not concerned about your biological clock?"

"I can't believe we're having this conversation. The truth is the only clock which concerns me is the one which wakes me up in the morning. I like my life. Among other advantages, it's nice to sleep through the night without being awakened to tend to someone else's needs. Now take your best shot."

"What's that?"

"Accuse me of being selfish and self-centered."

"Actually there've been a few nights when I'd

probably agree with you. But what about a lover awakening you to cuddle?''

''I thought we were talking about children.''

''You were the one bringing up sleeping undisturbed. Sounds like someone used to sleeping alone.''

''Who I sleep with is—''

''Out! Out!'' Ashley shrieked, rescuing Mackie from completing her answer. The baby's rebellion against the car seat and tearful whining and crying consumed Gordon's attentions during the rest of the drive.

The crying didn't abate until they arrived back at Mackie's. Worn from her tantrum, Ashley settled into her makeshift crib, stuck her thumb into her mouth and fell sound asleep. Mackie stared down at the little girl, amazed this could be the same impossible child of moments ago and thinking how enchanting she looked in sleep, how lovable. For the first time in ages, Mackie fantasized about having a baby of her own, then quickly shook her head, disowning such craziness.

Mackie had known for years who she was and what she wanted. Since her divorce, she'd devoted herself wholeheartedly to preparing herself for a career, then to ensuring that said career moved in an upward spiral. A bit of community service, a set of friends with the same goals. The pattern was set. *This was Mackie Smith.* Childless. Husbandless. And liking it that way.

Turning to Gordon, she said, ''I know better than to waste my time suggesting you go home. So you can read or watch TV. I'll be catching up on some paperwork in my study.''

"OK," Gordon said, "it's two-thirty now. Care to place a bet on when Beth gets here?''

Ignoring the jab, Mackie disappeared into her study.

Three, three-thirty, four. As she sat at her desk watching the time crawl by, Mackie gave thanks she hadn't risked a wager. She attempted to read and not listen for the doorbell, tapping her pen on the wooden desktop to fill the too-quiet room. It was useless. She couldn't concentrate.

Now she could hear Gordon talking to his daughter in the living room. How long would his patience hold before he bolted out with Ashley? Then again, perhaps he was enjoying the wait, knowing that with every passing second Mackie was twisting in the wind and that Beth's chances of winning shared custody were becoming as likely as world peace.

Finally at 4:32 the phone rang.

"Guess who?" Beth said.

"The woman who's an hour and a half late to pick up her child.''

"I know, I know," Beth agreed. "You have a right to be teed off at me, but Mackie, I'm still at the garage waiting for that part. The mechanic has promised to work late and get it fixed for me, but he can't make it before eight at the earliest.''

"Ashley will be asleep by then. You might as well wait and pick her up early tomorrow morning. By nine.''

Beth gave no argument. "Will do. And Mackie...?"

"Yes?"

"Thanks."

"Goodbye, Beth." Mackie punched off the phone. Why did she tell Beth to wait until morning? Was it genuine solicitousness about uprooting a sleeping Ashley? Or was she carving out more time for herself? The more she was around these two—father and daughter—the more involved she became. Not smart, Mackie, she told herself. But too late now—Beth would not be coming. Now all she had to do was tell Gordon.

CHAPTER THREE

STEELED for a celebratory round of "I told you so's," Mackie was astonished when Gordon made no smart-alecky cracks after she related the outcome of Beth's phone call.

"I see," he said, seemingly preoccupied with changing Ashley's diaper. Snapping the legs of her overalls, he sat on the couch and hoisted the child into his lap. "So what now?"

Mackie tucked her hair behind her ears. "I guess I can't offer much resistance if you insist on taking Ashley home for the night."

"No, I've heeded your warning about the judge and decided to follow his order as close as possible."

"And that means?"

"That I'll be using your couch again."

Once more Mackie was surprised. Surprised and grateful, too, not to have to play the role of stalwart defender. Gordon's predictions about Beth were coming terribly close to the mark and clouds of doubt as to her client's credibility massed in Mackie's head.

But she'd made the rules, and now she needed to see the evening through as best she could. Keep it simple, uncomplicated. Dinnertime was coming. She would focus on that.

"You might as well know that I don't cook," she told Gordon. "What do you say we run over to Eatzi's and pick up some takeout?"

"OK by me."

The forty-five minute trip took twice that long. Chalk up another Ashley excursion. Extra time to load and unload the baby from the car. Then in the market, pulling apples, candy and other delectables away from acquisitive little fingers, plus restacking a display of crackers. Ashley had snatched a box from the middle, collapsing the whole pile. Lumberjacking might be easier than caring for a young child, Mackie decided. And yet every time Ashley cast those round blue eyes her way or grinned her silly grin, the protective coating around Mackie's heart softened a millimeter more.

"This looks good," Gordon said, as he began removing containers from the sacks, lifting lids, then scooping some of the contents onto a plate for Ashley.

"Better than anything you'd get to eat at my house without the miracle of takeout," she said. "My last major experiment in the kitchen resulted in a visit from the Fire Department. Once the smoke cleared, one of the firemen suggested I consider turning in my apron permanently. Then for weeks, I had to endure the apartment reeking of burned rice. So now I undertake the occasional simple breakfast, but that's the extent of my culinary efforts."

If Gordon had been compiling personality profiles, he'd have felt safe in describing Mackie Smith as a perfectionist. Her meticulous dress, her everything-just-so furnishings, her need to win.

The hint of defiance in her tone just now told him it wasn't easy for her to confide a flaw. And yet she had. He stroked his chin. Interesting. Mackie might put heavy demands on herself but she obviously wasn't the automaton he'd made her out to be.

All-in-all, she'd been unbelievably flexible and accommodating considering the spot Beth had put her in. There was a lot more to Mackie than met the eye. He had never encountered a woman who intrigued him as she did.

"I can't believe she likes marinated artichokes," Mackie said, oblivious to Gordon's thoughts. She was leaning against the cabinet, sipping a glass of white wine as Gordon fed Ashley cubes of grilled chicken breast along with the artichokes and some cooked carrots.

When they'd arrived home and opened the food containers, Ashley had spotted the artichokes and demanded a bite. But rather than spitting it out as expected, she had wanted more.

"Who can account for children's tastes? She tried some at a Christmas party and has liked them ever since. And yet I can't get even one ordinary green bean into her." He fed her another tiny piece of chicken.

Regardless of her earlier opinion about Gordon, Mackie had to concede that he was a splendid parent.

She'd now spent almost twenty-four hours with father and daughter, and the evidence was impossible to ignore.

He might be contentious and unyielding in their legal clashes, but with Ashley, he was tender, loving, solicitous and fiercely protective. Not a single flaw surfaced in the way he cared for his daughter. And her mission?—to rip that child away from him. For the first time in her career, Mackie felt unsure of the rightness of her cause. It was much simpler back when the enemy had been faceless.

Once Ashley was fed, bathed and dressed for bed, Gordon and Mackie moved the playpen into Mackie's study so that the baby could sleep undisturbed while the adults ate.

Mackie heated their food in the microwave while Gordon poured himself a glass of wine and freshened hers. "I'll set the table," he offered, pulling silverware from a drawer.

Here we go again, Mackie told herself. The second night in a row acting as if we're a family when we're anything but. They'll never believe this down at the office. And Gordon's attorneys will be turning cartwheels when they find out.

But what was done was done and all the handwringing in the world about how this would look to others wouldn't change the situation. Better to enjoy this delicious food and worry about facing the consequences later.

She joined him at the table with their dinners and they ate silently. "What made you decide to become a professor?'' she asked, attempting to fill the conversational void.

''Mainly so I could have time for my family. My father was a heart surgeon and we seldom saw him. Work, work, work. I can't recall him making a single Little League game or being around to share birthday parties. I decided I wasn't going to raise my children like that.

''Fortunately I genuinely love what I do, combining some writing with the teaching. The money isn't great, not in my field anyway, but there's some prestige when you're associated with a major university. The best part is I'm able to control my own schedule...aside from classes and some office hours to meet with students, I can work from home. That means plenty of quality time with Ashley. It's a good life.''

''I envy you that...I mean the flexibility. The major part of my time is spent chained to a desk or trapped in a courtroom.''

''But all for a good cause, right...defending helpless mothers?'' His tone was sarcastic as if he equated all helpless mothers with Beth.

Mackie bristled. Every time she dared to relax around him, he sprang to the attack again. ''Yes, I do spend a lot of hours defending helpless mothers,'' she huffed. ''There *are* plenty out there you know.''

''Of course I know. I even realize that it's generally the mother on the short end of the stick after a divorce. But Beth's not one of them.''

''Really? Well, a professor's pay may not be great

but it's a whole lot better than what Beth earns working in a restaurant. Plus she doesn't have a big inheritance to fall back on. Not like some people I know."

"Aha. Now we're back at the core of the matter. Money."

"That's not what I meant."

"Sure sounded that way."

"Then I misspoke."

"Hmm. A lawyer misspeaking. That's a scary thought."

She rose and scraped the remains of her meal into the garbage disposal. "If you're through eating, why don't we take our coffee and dessert and see what's on television."

One of the networks was showing a movie neither had seen. The film, a romantic comedy, helped to ease the flare-up from dinner. Also, it set off a jumble of emotions in Mackie. It was fun to hear Gordon's deep-throated laughter and she liked the movie's humor, too. But the romantic parts created a self-consciousness and made her all too aware that seated close to her was a desirable male.

Gordon rested an arm across the back of the couch and a couple of times touched her shoulder to point out something on the screen or make a comment. And every time he touched her, she couldn't suppress a flutter within. For goodness' sake, she was worse than a rock star fan palpitating over being in the company of her idol. The man was not making moves on her and yet she was reacting as if he were.

That did it. Tomorrow he had to go—with or without Ashley. She was stretching the limits of ethics to the maximum already with this cozy little threesome. A few hours more with Gordon and she might as well turn in her license to practice law.

The movie ended and commercials for the ten o'clock news came on. Time to make excuses and get away while the getting was good. Mackie began clearing the coffee cups and Gordon rose to help. Once that was done, she bid a hasty good-night and started up the stairs.

Gordon watched as Mackie left the room. *Fled* is more like it, he thought. A man could get a complex from her avoidance techniques—the way she took such pains to escape his presence or, if she wasn't doing that, trying to run him off. Sure she had a legal responsibility not to establish a relationship with him. But there was no danger of that. No danger at all.

He tiptoed into the study to check on Ashley, the night-light casting shadows on her cherubic face. With her plump little body and red-footed fleece pajamas, she resembled a Teletubby. When he saw her like this, his heart grew so full he could hardly stand it. No man could love a child more than he loved Ashley. And, as he'd told Mackie and his own lawyers, he would do whatever it took not to lose her.

Returning to the living room, he plopped down on the couch. As much as he wanted to despise Mackie for what she was trying to do to him and Ashley, his heart told him that Mackie Smith wasn't simply a ruthless lawyer who'd been attacking him willy-nilly, but a caring counselor who misguidedly believed she was aiding a loving mother. Still, it was that very dedication of hers that made him lash out as he did and fight the compulsion to shake some sense into her.

A display of basketball scores on the TV screen drew his attention for a moment, but only for a moment, as his mind jumped back to Mackie. Not since Beth had won him over with her siren's call had a woman monopolized his interest as Mackie did. Her beauty, her ambition, her sexy—

You must be the biggest fool in Dallas, Galloway. Maybe all that education he'd gotten had played havoc with his common sense. How else could he explain being drawn to the wrong woman—twice in a row? First Beth, a female with all the scruples of a purse snatcher, and now Mackie, a woman who not only couldn't stand too much of his company, but who had every intention of tearing him to shreds in court. All he was missing was a Kick Me sign on his back.

Disgusted with himself, Gordon grabbed the remote control and began channel surfing, determined to find a program that would hold his attention or put him to sleep. He didn't care which.

When Mackie came downstairs at seven the next morning, Gordon was curled up on the couch, one of his arms hanging over the edge, fingertips touching the floor. His shirt and pants were draped over a chair and a black T-shirt was visible above the blanket that had slipped to his waist.

She hastened to the kitchen. Coffee was beginning to drip into the carafe by the time she heard Ashley stir. Mackie started after her only to meet Gordon who'd beaten her to the study where Ashley was. He had not taken the time to dress and was wearing only the T-shirt and matching briefs.

"Oh…" Her eyes did a quick sweep of his long muscular legs before she turned away. Now this would really make a great story for the office. Only no one was ever going to hear it. Probably not even her best friend, Taurika.

"Sorry," he said, acknowledging his state of undress. "Didn't realize you were up. Must have been dead asleep." *Especially after tossing and turning half the night, trying to banish certain erotic thoughts from my head.*

"No problem. I'll just slip back into the kitchen while the two of you get…uh…presentable." She beat a hasty exit. Amazing she told herself. Gordon could sleep through her coming downstairs and puttering in the kitchen. Yet the minute his daughter moved, he sprang to life. A parent's special instinct she guessed.

"Does Ashley like scrambled eggs?" she said, her voice a croak as the image of Gordon in his briefs replayed in her brain. As Gordon entered the kitchen with Ashley in his arms, Mackie determinedly kept her gaze on Ashley even though Gordon was now fully clothed.

"Nope, she's strictly a cereal person. But I do. Need any help?"

"No, you'll probably have your hands full keeping Ashley out of harm's way. As you're aware, this is not a childproof kitchen."

Gordon held Ashley as she ate bananas and Cheerios and Mackie cooked a basic breakfast—eggs, toast and coffee. "Julia Child would be aghast," she said, placing a plate in front of him. "No diced truffles or fresh herbs."

"Nonsense. Julia Child likes good food and this looks darn good." He proceeded to verify his statement by giving Ashley a bite of toast and then by wolfing down the eggs.

They ate quietly and quickly, only Ashley filling the silence with baby chatter.

Patting her mouth with a paper napkin, Mackie looked over at the stove clock. Quarter after eight. She couldn't postpone this any longer. "Beth will be here soon. I think you should leave before she arrives," she told Gordon.

When Gordon started to protest, Mackie continued, bolstering her argument. "What will it accomplish if you two get into a fracas in front of Ashley?"

He grimaced. "Give me a little credit here. I'm—"

"Please just do this. You're due to get Ashley back today anyway."

"OK," he said reluctantly, standing up. "But since I'm being hustled out so early, can I at least have one for the road?'' He was holding up the coffee carafe. ''I always have two cups in the morning to start my day.''

Mackie rose and rummaged through the pantry. Finding a stack of Styrofoam cups, she handed one to him. After he filled it, she and Ashley walked him to the door.

''Well, sweetie,'' he said to the baby, ''Daddy has to go bye-bye for a while. Your...your...Beth will be here to play with you, and Mackie will play with you too.'' He kissed the baby's cheeks and forehead.

Ashley rubbed his face, giggling at the feel of his morning beard. He kissed her again, a peck on the lips.

''Kist,'' Ashley said, pointing at Mackie.

''Uh-uh,'' Gordon said. ''All my kisses are for you, pumpkin.''

''Kist,'' Ashley persisted. Again she pointed at Mackie.

Gordon bent over and kissed Mackie on the forehead. A whiff of perfume, some unidentifiable floral mixture...jasmine, frangipani...enveloped him. He quickly pulled away.

Still not satisfied, Ashley insisted, ''Here.'' She pointed to Mackie's mouth.

Flustered, Gordon gave Mackie a peck on the lips similar to the one he'd bestowed on Ashley. As he pulled away, he whispered, ''I'm only doing this to placate my daughter, you know.''

''Of course, I know.''

He said goodbye, ruffled Ashley's hair, then trotted down the sidewalk toward his car. *Like hell I was kissing her just for Ashley.* He could still smell Mackie's perfume. Another time, a different scenario, and he would have wrapped her in his arms and kissed her for real. Blame it on close quarters, but the notion of her as an adversary was becoming more unpalatable by the minute. "Remember Ashley, remember Ashley," he whispered to himself.

Breezing in at eleven-thirty, long past her agreed-upon arrival, Beth patted her daughter's cheek. "Hello, my darling baby," she cooed to Ashley in her playpen.

"Mackie, I must apologize again. My alarm didn't go off."

Mackie didn't bother to respond.

"Are you mad at me?"

"Don't even ask. Just help me get her stuff."

The two women began gathering up belongings and by the time all the baby gear had been loaded into Beth's Honda and she and Ashley had driven away, it was noon.

Alone now in her town house, Mackie was taken aback by the eerie silence. This was the first time in two days she'd been totally by herself and she felt a resounding loneliness, an entirely new sensation for someone who lived alone and up until now had liked it.

For Mackie, a normal Sunday in February meant snuggling into bed with a big cup of coffee and the oversize edition of the *Dallas Morning News*. Often, still exhausted from a strenuous work week, she would nod off.

Today, however, she couldn't concentrate on the newspaper, and there was no nodding off, either. She'd been troubled at allowing Beth to leave with Ashley. *What if something happens to her?* Mackie gave a quick little shake to her head. She needed to get hold of herself. After all, the baby girl was reunited with her mother. Precisely what Mackie had been working for all these weeks. Frustrated, she rose and began organizing her closet to occupy her hands and her mind.

At five, her doorbell rang. "Hope you don't object to my coming early," Gordon said. "It's been a long, torturous day."

It had been for Mackie as well. "Beth's not due for another hour."

"I know. I can wait in the car if you prefer."

"Don't be silly. Come inside. There's still some wine from last night. Would you like a glass—or maybe a beer?"

"No, thanks. I'll have Ash on the ride home. No drinking and driving when she's with me."

"A Coke then?"

"Sure."

Now that he'd had a few hours away from Mackie to give himself a good talking to, Gordon was chagrined at fantasizing about this woman last night. He felt ill at ease in her company. Why hadn't he just waited in the car? Because the notion of him outside and her inside heightened his discomfort. He had this compulsive need to be around her, darn it.

He couldn't help wishing things were different. He hadn't cared about a woman in so long he'd almost forgotten the way it felt. Being with Mackie had reminded him. But all it did was confuse him totally.

At five-fifteen, the bell rang again. "I didn't want to be late," Beth said, entering with Ashley.

The baby immediately reached for her father.

"Hello, Gordon," Beth said. "We had a good weekend together."

Who do you think you're kidding? A long silence followed as Gordon fought the urge to tell Beth he knew how few hours she'd actually spent with Ashley. But what would be gained by causing a scene? Ashley was back in his arms again—and the deck was definitely stacked in his favor. "Well, we'd better be going," Gordon finally said to Mackie. "The Galloways have taken up entirely too much of your weekend as it is." Going outside, the three transferred Ashley's paraphernalia from Beth's car to Gordon's van.

"See you in two weeks, honey bunch," Beth said to Ashley, waving her fingers as Gordon began loading the little girl into her car seat.

Gordon did not try to mask his disgust.

"Well, I *will*," Beth taunted. "Whether you like it or not."

Mackie wished Beth would keep her mouth shut. All she needed was a melee on her front walk. But Gordon managed to control his temper and didn't rise to Beth's bait. Once Ashley was secured in the back of the van, he climbed in and drove away.

"Don't be so sure about that next visit," Mackie answered on his behalf, once Gordon was out of sight.

"What do you mean by that?"

"Come back inside and I'll tell you."

Beth flopped down on the sofa and Mackie sat on the arm of a chair, and for the next ten minutes she relayed what had transpired since Friday.

"I didn't say she could be with you *and* Gordon," Beth criticized. "You shouldn't have called him." She stood up, hands on hips, locking eyes with Mackie.

Mackie returned stare for stare. "You gave me no choice. I was afraid Ashley was sick. I told you that—but you hung up as if it was nothing."

"You're right," Beth said, contrition in her voice. "I was inconsiderate. You have every right to hate me. It's just that—"

Mackie didn't want to hear her excuses. "I don't hate you, Beth, I simply want you to see things as they are. It wasn't just Friday, you know. Apparently playing Mommy hasn't been convenient for you most of the weekend. The car stuff I can understand, but oversleeping this morning?

"Frankly, I have to wonder whether you've been feeding me a tale. If so, that's a dumb thing to do with one's attorney. Now sit down and listen to what I have to tell you."

Beth hesitated.

"I said sit down!"

Beth flinched, then sat as commanded.

Mackie regretted being so sharp, but it was for Beth's own good. She needed to listen, *really* listen. Mackie joined her on the sofa and laid out how this turn of events might affect their case.

"Your work problems and car problems and the way you handled them played right into their hands. By shunting your daughter onto me, you've opened up the fitness question, the very thing we were trying to overcome. And Gordon got a front row seat where he could witness every turn of events."

"So what do we do now?" Beth asked. "Throw in the towel...give up?"

I wish. But Mackie was the consummate professional. Screwups aside, she was still Beth's attorney, still obligated to do the best by her client. "No, the ball's in their court. We just wait and see."

"So how did things go with the battling Galloways?" Taurika Stokes asked as Mackie arrived at work Monday morning. Taurika was not only Mackie's best friend, but a fellow attorney at her firm.

"Not too good."

"Hope this doesn't make it worse." She handed Mackie a message slip from Sonia Mott, Gordon's lawyer.

"Doesn't say what she wants, but I doubt she's calling just for a bit of girl talk," Mackie said. "If you have a minute, I'll fill you in." The two went to Mackie's office where, desperate to share her feelings, she related the events of the last three days.

At the end of Mackie's tale, Taurika threw her palms up. "Help me out here. Just a week ago you had the guy on a par with Hitler. Now you're beginning to sound sympathetic to him. Quite a turnaround, wouldn't you say?"

Mackie couldn't exactly believe it herself. "I know I've changed my tune, but remember, most of my information about him came from Beth. But after the weekend..." Mackie sighed. "He's not exactly the devil incarnate like Beth described. And she's not the poor little victim of circumstances she made herself out to be. I'm pretty sure her desperate mother act is just that, an act. It's beginning to look like I've been taken for a ride."

Taurika patted her hand. "It happens."

"Not to me."

"Then you were long overdue. Honestly, girl, you've always been a pushover for a hard-luck story."

"Thanks a lot," Mackie grumped.

"Don't get all bent out of shape—that's one of the things people love about you. You don't find many bleeding hearts in our profession these days."

"I didn't know everyone considered me a bleeding heart. Makes me wonder how many other clients have taken me in. Have I let my own poor excuse for a marriage cloud my judgment about other peoples' relationships?"

"Why do you seem intent on beating yourself up?

It's one case—'' Taurika smiled knowingly. "Hmm...tell me more about Galloway."

Mackie leaned back in her desk chair. "Not much to tell except that Gordon's beginning to rank a lot higher on the trustworthiness scale than his former wife."

"Oh I got that part, but could you throw in a few facts?"

"The facts are he's got recent wealth from an inheritance, has a Ph.D. and teaches at the university. What I've observed firsthand is that he's devoted to his daughter, is quite good-looking and at times has all the finesse of a collection agent."

"Good-looking, huh?"

"Taurika, were you listening to the other stuff? The man is trouble in a fancy package."

"A little trouble? That's all that's disturbing you? You complain about being sold a bill of goods by Beth, but is that what's making you edgy, or is it because you've gone soft for a legal foe who happens to be easy on the eyes?"

"I've done no such thing—"

"Course not."

"Gordon Galloway is everything I don't want in a man. Divorced with a child. Why...the guy's Mr. Mom. Domesticity with a capital *D*."

"Methinks the lady doth protest too much."

"Excuse me," their secretary interrupted, rescuing Mackie from Taurika's inquisition. "This just came for you, Mackie." She handed over an express delivery envelope.

Mackie opened the envelope, scanned the contents and shrieked, ''That...that rat!'' She shook the papers in front of Taurika's face. ''Now I know what Sonia was phoning about...she didn't even give me time to get back to her. And Galloway...so much for his being trustworthy. He's petitioning the court to set aside the temporary visitation.''

CHAPTER FOUR

"Hang on a sec." Taurika "teed" her hands into a time-out signal. "Are you trying to tell me you weren't expecting this?"

"I *expected* Galloway to use what he'd learned as leverage. I *didn't expect* him to charge back into court without giving me a...a..." Mackie sighed and looked up at Taurika. "Don't bother saying it...I'm being irrational."

A shrug was Taurika's response.

Mackie tossed the brief on her desk and squeezed the bridge of her nose with her fingertips. Galloway's lawyers had targeted Beth's sins of omission, citing her various failures to be with Ashley on Friday and Saturday as signs of a bigger pattern.

Mackie looked up at Taurika. "This proves it. I'm a certified idiot." All weekend she'd thought she'd been learning about Galloway...beginning to see his side of the story, starting to actually like the guy. And to believe he liked her. Yet all the while, he'd been amassing information about Beth's activities and nefariously plotting how to turn this ill-gotten knowledge to his advantage.

"Well, as a lawyer, I can't fault his strategy," Taurika said.

"Me, neither, darn it." She might try to appear a

good sport to Taurika, but at her core, Mackie
couldn't help but feel betrayed. Even while preparing
Beth for dire consequences ahead, some part of
Mackie had naively hoped that Gordon might not do
what anyone with a grain of smarts would do—act on
the weekend's events. Stupid of her thinking like
that—only some idealistic rookie would make that
mistake.

And taking Gordon's action as a personal affront
was illogical at best. But logic didn't change the fact
she was disappointed...hurt...angry.

Probably just as well, too. She needed to hang onto
those feelings. Gordon was the opposition and she'd
gotten entirely too cozy and empathetic. But no more.

Given her druthers, she'd grab the telephone and
tell Gordon just what she thought of his methods.
"His commitment to his daughter has never been in
doubt," she said to Taurika. "And I was so taken in
by fatherly devotion—" *Not to mention dazzled by
his male attraction.* "—that I let my guard drop. But
Gordon never forgot we were adversaries. Not for a
second."

"So what are you going to do now?"

"As much as I'd like to ventilate to him personally,
I suppose I'll have to take the old-fashioned proce-
dural route." Mackie was all too aware that ethical
boundaries had been seriously breached already. If
she called and confronted Gordon the way she wanted
to, there'd be no excusing her behavior, her judgment.

"Good girl." Taurika rose. "Want to go to lunch
later? You can ventilate to me instead of Gordon."

"Thanks, but I'd better stay in. Especially with this unexpected work to take care of." Mackie tapped a fingernail on the hot-off-the-press Galloway petition. "I'll probably just snack on some cheese and crackers at my desk."

"OK, but if you change your mind, you know where to find me."

"You're a pal."

As Taurika left, Mackie reached for a legal pad and began scribbling notes for herself before she tried to reach Sonia. It was a daunting task. Every dratted accusation they would present about Beth would be true. All Mackie had to offer were mitigating circumstances. And she knew that would cut no ice with Gordon, and probably not with a judge.

She felt terrible. Despite Beth's machinations, Mackie knew the main blame for this current debacle lay at her own feet. She'd put the events in motion with that panicky Friday night call. By phoning Galloway, she'd opened Pandora's box, given him access to details he might never have gotten without her. As a result, she'd put her client's best interests in jeopardy. She might no longer be the blind ally she once was for Beth, but that didn't change her obligations to protect her at all costs.

Recriminations aside, she needed to touch base with Sonia. But not in this frame of mind, Mackie cautioned herself. Why rush into a confrontation when she was mad as a hornet? She needed to let the dust settle and gather her wits about her. Later in the morning would be soon enough.

But when Mackie placed the call at eleven, Sonia was out. They played telephone tag the rest of the day with Mackie finally finding out that Sonia had left for a trial in Houston and wouldn't return until the next Monday.

The Galloway case didn't temporarily cease to exist because of Sonia's absence, however. Gordon himself phoned three times Monday afternoon, but Mackie dodged his calls, telling her secretary not to put him through. When he caught her at home that evening, she made short shrift of the discussion.

"Mackie, I need to explain—"

"I don't need your explanations and—not that you've ever given a darn—our talking isn't proper."

"Back to the rule book, are you?"

"Mock me if it'll make you feel better, but I talk to your attorney and no one else. If she's ever available that is. Sonia's office told me she's away until next week. Beth and I want this settled. But until Sonia gets in touch, we're in a holding pattern."

"We can work this out," Gordon protested.

"Can we? If so, why didn't I hear from you before you headed back to court?"

"I was only looking out for Ashley. I didn't mean—"

"Say no more," Mackie snarled, cutting him off. "If Sonia ever makes herself available, I'll talk to her. For the gazillionth time, conversations between us are inappropriate, so don't call me again." She hung up before he could utter another word.

Over the next few days, Gordon picked up the re-

ceiver half a dozen times to call, but he didn't.
Mackie had set the terms and this time, he was taking
her at her word. But that didn't mean he had to like
it. Why couldn't the woman be reasonable? Surely
she could see the latest legal maneuver wasn't personal. He'd simply had no choice.

Mackie was spending those same days striving to
regain her equilibrium. She did it by burying herself
in work, dispensing with the multitude of chores her
busy caseload demanded. Negotiating a settlement for
one brawling divorce couple, three days in court on
a second.

Yet the daily calls from Beth made Mackie feel as
if she were falling two steps backward for every one
she took forward. "Any word yet?" Beth would ask,
and with each "no" become more irrational.

"This is your fault, you know, Mackie. I should
have hired a male lawyer, someone who could stand
up to Gordon."

"You didn't *hire* anyone, Beth. You got me for
free." *Sap that I am.* "But if you feel like throwing
your hard-earned dollars around, I'll be glad to pro-
vide some names."

"No, no, I shouldn't have said that. I'm sorry. It's
just that all this has me so uptight."

You and me both, kiddo. "I'll call you as soon as
I hear anything, Beth. Bye now." The next day it was
more of the same.

When Harris Nelson asked Mackie to attend a
Friday night gallery showing, she readily said yes,
grateful for the distraction. Harris was one of her ilk,

a physician as committed to his cardiology practice as she was to family law. Although she didn't date often, when she went out, generally Mackie was paired with him.

The gallery was near downtown, off Cedar Springs, and already bustling with people when they entered. "A good crowd," Mackie commented as Harris handed her a glass of champagne.

"The featured artist, Anton Garza, is a favorite of mine. What do you think of this one?" Harris pointed to a floor-to-ceiling canvas with splashes of gray paint.

Mackie tilted her head this way and that, evaluating the painting. "I think I prefer Monet. At least I know what I'm looking at."

Harris laughed. "Your imagination needs to be primed, that's all. A hundred years from now critics may be comparing Anton's works to the masters. Did you catch his write-up in last Friday's newspaper?"

"No, I missed it."

That particular day had begun one of the most difficult periods in Mackie's career. She vowed not to think about it, especially when such thoughts led straight to Gordon Galloway. Round two of the controversy was on next week's agenda; she'd save it until then. However, as often as Mackie tried to force her mind to comply, she hadn't found it easy to relegate Gordon to the future.

And why, for pity's sake? So he was handsome, and pleasant when everything went his way. But she had to keep his perfidy foremost in her thoughts. That was the only way she could maintain some sort of balance. Unless she stoked her fury, Mackie found herself entertaining ridiculous reveries of Gordon. It had to stop—they could never be a couple. A relationship between them was forbidden fruit because of their status—lawyer and opposing client.

Add to that the fact she was on the fast track with her career, and he, admittedly, was happy just where he was. Gordon Galloway led the very life she'd decided to have no part of. House...child... Why... Mackie realized with a start that Harris was speaking to her.

"...a copy around here somewhere," he was saying. "Let me scrounge one up for you."

"Oh, the article, of course...thanks."

Harris went off in search and Mackie began examining a large oil painting mounted nearby. It was purple and black, and was anyone's guess as to what the artist intended. *Is it me or is that the ugliest thing I've ever seen?*

"Man, that's the ugliest thing I've ever seen," muttered a male guest next to her.

Mackie laughed and turned to address the person who'd voiced her very reaction... *Oh my.* It was the man she'd been thinking of only moments ago. Gordon Galloway in the flesh, as if she'd conjured him up. The flutter in her stomach reignited all her suppressed rage.

"Oh," she said frostily, "I didn't see you standing there." It took all of Mackie's willpower not to go on the attack then and there, only a sense of decorum keeping her temper in check.

"Obviously not or you'd be sprinting off in the other direction to avoid me."

He might be as surprised by the chance encounter as she, but it didn't take long for Gordon to start sniping. Not fair when she couldn't properly reciprocate.

To make matters worse, tonight Gordon was even more attractive than usual. She liked the hip image— black leather jacket and black turtleneck sweater. He was dressed as if he had a Harley-Davidson parked outside. Too bad Galloway's desperado handsomeness sat on the shoulders of such a treacherous male. He didn't even have the good grace to look shamefaced.

Mackie would have given a week's pay to avoid this accidental meeting. As much as she longed to have her say, she wasn't prepared for a face-to-face encounter. Too many feelings pulled at her when he got close.

But too late to escape now and the scene called for a semblance of civility. She couldn't go for his jugular in the midst of this culture-seeking crowd. A few words of innocuous small talk, then she'd move on. "Not a fan of Anton Garza I take it," she said.

"Actually Anton is a friend of mine. He mentioned the opening and I promised to stop by."

"Does he know you're here trashing his work? He might want to withdraw the invitation."

"Friend or not, that thing's an abomination,"

Gordon said. "I tell him all the time his work's hideous."

"And he doesn't take offense?"

"No. Claims he would be upset if I weren't so ignorant about art. Says I might be able to write books but artistically all my taste is in my mouth. And I guess he's right—the critics think he's wonderful in spite of my opinion."

Mackie gave a polite titter, took a fortifying swallow of champagne, then the couple stood side by side uncomfortably scoping out the room as a lengthy pause ensued.

"Listen Mackie…" Gordon began. Just then Harris returned.

"The newspaper article's making the rounds," Harris said to Mackie. Looking at Gordon he extended a hand. "Sorry if I interrupted. Harris Nelson. I don't believe we've met."

"Gordon Galloway."

"He's a friend of the artist," Mackie said.

Harris's face lit up. "Terrific. Maybe you'd be kind enough to make introductions. I'd like to meet him. Got my eye on that still life near the entrance. It'll go great in my waiting room."

Gordon and Mackie cast their eyes toward a red-and-black oil. It was every bit as bold and audacious as the one they'd been disparaging. "You must be an art connoisseur," Gordon said to Harris. "I couldn't tell it *was* a still life."

Harris chuckled good-naturedly. "It seems you

have about as much appreciation for his work as Mackie does.''

"Harris, that particular painting could cause your patients to *develop* heart trouble if they didn't have it already,'' Mackie said.

"Shall I put it in front of my office then? To drum up business? I might need to, because the purchase will make a sizable dent in the old Visa balance.'' Harris patted his wallet just as his pager beeped. "My answering service. Excuse me while I check in.'' He pulled out a tiny cellular phone and headed for a quiet corner.

"Nice guy,'' Gordon commented when Harris walked off.

"Yes, he is.'' Mackie fiddled with her earring. She was stuck here waiting for Harris. Why wouldn't Gordon just go away? Pretending there was no tension between them was excruciating.

"Listen, about the motion,'' he began again. "I wish you'd let me explain.''

"As a friend of the artist don't you need to mingle...talk up Anton's work?'' It was pointless for Gordon to try to weasel out of what he'd done. The gallery might be neutral turf, but their differences were definitely partisan, as he'd confirmed to her regret. And this wasn't the place to get into them.

Gordon's jaw tensed. Mackie Smith was the most impossible, pigheaded woman. He'd tried to make her understand Monday on the phone but she wouldn't take his calls, wouldn't listen when he finally reached her at home. She was acting as if he'd stabbed her in the back. And maybe he had. Sort of. But since when did lawsuits fall into the realm of civilized or courtly behavior.

Anyway, as a lawyer, Mackie should be willing and able to compartmentalize the legal part and the...the other part.

But since he'd been so effectively dismissed, he damn sure didn't intend to keep begging her for an audience. He was moving away when Harris returned, phone in hand.

"Mackie, I've got an emergency," he announced. "Need to get to the hospital as soon as possible."

"The perils of dating a doctor," she said, unperturbed.

"I feel rotten leaving you stranded."

"Don't worry. I'm perfectly capable of getting myself home. I'll just call a taxi."

Harris made a face. "I'm not wild about that idea...say—" He clasped Gordon's shoulder. "Galloway, can you do me a favor? See that Mackie gets home?"

"See her home?" Gordon could already hear Mackie's reaction to that suggestion; nevertheless, he was going to take the gentlemanly route. "Be glad to."

"I'd appreciate that. Well, good night. I'll call you tomorrow, Mackie."

As Harris left, Mackie glared at his departing back. Harris had a nerve. Dallas's taxi service might not be perfect, but that didn't give him license to palm her off on the handiest male. And Galloway of all people.

Harris could have lobbed a dart into the air and hit anyone more suitable than Gordon Galloway to chauffeur her home.

"You really don't have to drive me," she said. "I don't mind a taxi. In fact I'd prefer a taxi."

Gordon shook his head. "I'm sure you would, but I promised Harris. He would be less than happy with me to discover I didn't mean it. This will salve his conscience at leaving you."

Mackie started to protest further, but conceded that making a fuss would only create public dissension. It was a car ride, that was all. She'd managed to hold her tongue thus far, surely she could hang on for the thirty minutes it would take to drive from the gallery to her place. "Since you put it that way."

"Before we go, though, I need to speak to Anton. How about meeting the artist you're so fond of?" There was a devilish twinkle in Gordon's eyes.

"Sure. Only give me a minute to come up with something nice to say about his work first."

"A minute?" Gordon cocked an eyebrow. "That could take hours. But it'll probably be a spell before we can get through his crowd of admirers anyway. Would you like more champagne?"

Actually she could swill a whole magnum, but Mackie shook her head. She was having enough difficulty keeping her wits about her as it was.

After wending their way through the knots of people, Gordon introduced Mackie to Anton, who looked the antithesis of a painter. A large hulk of a man, he appeared to devote more hours to lifting weights than to lifting brushes. No brooding artist type, either, but a sunny, hale-fellow-well-met kind of guy who gave Gordon grief for being housebound all the time and not getting out more.

Gordon offered to buy one of Anton's paintings if he'd get off his back. "Have to hang it in the garage, though, or it will give Ashley nightmares."

"Why?" Anton razzed. "Is she like her dad—afraid of good art?"

After a few more minutes of genial give and take between the friends, Gordon and Mackie moved away, yielding to the other guests who were demanding a visit with the artist.

"Ready to leave?" Gordon said to Mackie.

She nodded, but in truth she wasn't. Not like she was before. She'd been caught up in Gordon's banter with Anton, momentarily dropping her ire as she was reminded that her prickly companion could actually be fun to be around. *Forget it, Mackie,* she quickly admonished.

Gordon led the way out to his van. Noticing the child's car seat revived Mackie's agitation. Ashley...the custody case...her ambivalent feelings about Ashley's father. The only safe thing to do was to clamp her lips together and treat everything relating to the lawsuit as a taboo subject.

Once both of them had gotten in and shut the doors, Mackie realized how perfectly alone they were. Gordon must have been aware of the same thing, because for a few seconds there was a silence so pervasive the sound of their breathing was audible.

"Before you say anything..." he began.

"I wasn't going to say anything."

"Come on, I know you're dying to let me have it."

"With both barrels. But I'm not going to."

"OK, I'll do the talking. And please just do me the courtesy of listening."

"Do I have an alternative?"

He took her hand. "Mackie, I did what I had to do."

"Thanks for clearing that up," she said sarcastically, yanking the hand away, then frowning at him as if he were a bug she was studying under a magnifying glass.

"I didn't set out to entrap you or Beth. If she'd showed up later Friday night, or even Saturday, I probably wouldn't have asked Sonia to go back to court."

"Right."

"I told you I'd do whatever it took to hang on to Ashley. Friday's car mishap might have been genuine, but all day Saturday and Saturday night? Even you could see what was happening. Beth doesn't give a hoot about Ashley. If she did, she could have asked you to come get her Saturday so she could be with Ash...a loving mother would have thought of some way to be with her child. True?"

"I can't answer that." Actually there was but one answer and they both knew it. Everything he'd said *was* true. Stumped for a retort, Mackie turned away from him and began to stare out the window.

There was a distinct chill inside the car as Gordon headed down Cedar Springs toward Turtle Creek. This drive could be unbearably long if Mackie's cold shoulder extended for the duration. But he didn't mind leaning on her a bit harder. She deserved it. And it was better than enduring the stultifying quiet.

"Not a good feeling, is it?" he asked. "Bet you're hating yourself for buying into Beth's cause so easily—"

Her head spun around. "What do you mean easily? It's not like after a ten minute chat, I decided to start launching motions on her behalf. We spent hours and hours talking, and I took her case because I believed in her."

"Do you still—after serving as her unpaid baby-sitter most of the weekend? Has it crossed your mind that Beth had only about nine hours total with Ashley? She didn't come back early Sunday afternoon because she was concerned about being late—she came back because she'd had all the responsibility she could stomach."

Nine hours, ha—it was barely six. But Mackie wasn't about to tell Mr. Know-it-all that. "Call me gullible if it makes you feel better, but remember...I only represent her. You on the other hand *married* her."

"That's not the same."

"Face it, Galloway, if you think I've been sweet-talked and double-dealed by Beth, then it has to go quadruple for you. And that probably tees you off as much as the fact of her deserting you and Ashley."

"You don't know what you're talking about."

"Oh, no? Usually I'm pretty good at reading people."

"Yeah," he jeered, "you read Beth really well."

So much for trying to best him. They were back where they started. "Like you, I've done what I had to do—don't bother trying to make me feel guilty."

"So you just wash your hands of the situation and walk away with a clear conscience. Must be nice."

"I'm not walking anywhere. I'm still Beth's attorney and if you're asking me to get down on my knees and plead for your forgiveness because you think my enthusiasm is misplaced, then you're going to be disappointed. I'm doing my job, Mr. Galloway. And nothing more."

"So what do you and Beth plan to do about the motion?"

"That's for us to know and you to find out," Mackie quipped, knowing she sounded childish, but not especially caring. "Now, how about some nice music instead of this meaningless bickering?" She pushed the cassette player button and Barney the dinosaur came on singing "I love you..." She pushed the cassette off. "Never mind."

Silence reigned again, and this time, Gordon made no effort to alleviate it. He had half a mind to drop his passenger off at the nearest convenience store and tell her to call that taxi after all. No wonder so many people hated lawyers. Always playing God and acting as if they were smarter than everyone else. And Mackie was a lawyer all the way from the top of her perfectly coiffed head to those polished toenails peeking out from her evening sandals.

Sure, Beth had fooled him. Turned his head with her tight jeans and her stories of hard times, impressed him with how she was struggling to better her lot in life. He didn't know at the time that she brought most of her troubles on herself. He only saw her grit and determination to overcome the hurdles before her.

She was so sweet and lovable then and he had fallen harder than an old cottonwood tree in a spring storm. How in the world could Mackie Smith compare that to Beth's blatant manipulation of her? As he'd just told her, it was not the same.

Gordon had pulled up in front of Mackie's town house. "Good night, Mr. Galloway," she said, getting out. "Thanks for a lovely ride." She slammed the car door with all her might and marched up the sidewalk without a backward glance.

Gordon lingered in front of the town house, waiting to see that Mackie got in safely. "Duty's done. She's snug in her nest," he said aloud as the front door closed behind her. Shifting out of Park, he pulled away from the curb, thanking his lucky stars he didn't have to contend with Mackie Smith any more tonight. Right now he wished he'd never laid eyes on her.

Gordon arrived at his own house, bade the sitter good-night and stole a peek at his sleeping daughter. She was deep in dreamland, oblivious to his return home.

Removing his clothes, he went back downstairs and lay on the couch, first watching TV, then straining over a crossword puzzle. He tossed the folded newspaper aside and draped one arm over his eyes. As addled as he was from his "discussion" with Mackie Smith, he'd have difficulty coming up with a three-letter word for feline.

His fury had abated somewhat, but he was still unsettled. He tried to push Mackie from his thoughts with no success. She was embedded in his head like a splinter in the finger and just as pleasurable. Why did this female keep plaguing him, even when she wasn't here?

Tonight at the gallery she'd looked too darned sexy in that filmy floral top and skinny black velvet pants. *Especially those pants,* which set off a very nice derriere.

Perhaps his mother was right when she'd suggested that he needed to start dating. She'd intuited that he was deliberately avoiding intimacy with the opposite sex. Come to think of it, he'd spent more time interacting with female lawyers the past several weeks than he'd spent with any woman since Beth had walked out. A sad state of affairs, Galloway.

Probably the best way to oust the aggravating Ms. Smith from his mind was to put another woman in it. He'd gotten too far removed from male-female relationships. Gordon vowed then and there to extricate himself from this long-running womanless vacuum. Once this mess with Beth was over, he'd start forging some kind of a social life…whether he wanted to or not.

CHAPTER FIVE

PICKING up the telephone Saturday morning, Mackie punched in Taurika's number. She was going to cancel their planned outing to the Galleria for lunch and shopping. With a briefcase full of work and Gordon Galloway turning her world upside down, she was too upset to go anywhere. The Galloway case was weighing heavy on her, and try as she might, she couldn't get beyond it.

Mackie pushed the Off button and set the phone in the cradle. She was going about this all wrong. A day at the mall with shopping and gossipy talk would be much healthier than isolating herself with work and her misery. Now...what to wear?

"You look terrible," Taurika declared, setting her shopping bag under the table at the restaurant. "Come on, tell ole Dr. T what's wrong."

Why bore her friend? Especially when she couldn't satisfactorily explain what was eating at her. "Just tired, I guess."

"You need a vacation, girl. I picked up some brochures at American Express for that trip we keep promising ourselves. Look, here's a six-day package to Puerto Vallarta. We can lie on the beach, guzzle all kinds of fruity drinks and hunt for single men."

Mackie scanned the materials, trying to feign interest, but she couldn't muster any enthusiasm. Until she got Galloway et al off her back, she was worthless for trips or anything else and she knew it. She wasn't simply tired as she'd told Taurika. It was more than that.

"You have to take time to smell the roses," Taurika prattled on, oblivious to Mackie's inattention. "Every lawyer's billing caseload is grueling—if they're truly successful. And I know we're supposed to like it like that. But a busy caseload's one thing. You sign up for all those pro bonos, too, never give yourself room to play."

"True," Mackie answered lethargically. But it wasn't the degree of work that was taking its toll. She could handle working hard. The problem was her involvement with Gordon, an involvement that had strayed from the professional into the personal. This improper infatuation of hers was what was sapping her energy at a soul-draining rate.

"Mackie!" Taurika snapped her fingers. "Are you listening? I asked whether you thought we could both take off the same week?"

"Probably not," Mackie answered, glad for the excuse. Vacations didn't interest her at the moment. Her number one priority was regaining her sanity and getting her life back. First thing Monday morning she would call Sonia for an appointment.

"Do you even want to try?" Taurika said, then answered for her. "I can read your face and you're not with me here. I'll be glad when you've finally resolved whatever it is that's bothering you."

"What makes you think anything's bothering me?"

Taurika rolled her eyes. "To put it mildly, you haven't been yourself for weeks." Taurika took a sip of iced tea. "By my calculations the changes began about the time you met Gordon Galloway."

"If I've not been myself, it's because I'm spending too many of my off-hours absorbed with work. So let's head down to Nordstrom's and remedy that. Shopping is great therapy."

Gordon sat at the table in the conference room of Alexander, Mott and Percy, drumming his fingers against the polished wooden surface. "Are we clear, Sonia?" he asked his attorney who was seated across from him.

"You'd prefer not to take this to court," Sonia answered. "I get that. What I don't understand is why. We're guaranteed to come out on top this time, Gordon."

"Are we?" He removed his glasses and wiped them with a handkerchief as he spoke. "I recall your telling me we were guaranteed before and look what happened."

"Only because Mackie Smith pulled a fast one. She's not going to get away with any tricky stuff this—"

"I know I've got the best firm in Dallas, Sonia, but don't sell Mackie short. Not only is she smart, but she'll go to the mat for her client and her convictions. We need to be on our toes.''

Sonia scrunched her eyebrows together, then stood up and leaned across the desk, flattening her palms to steady her. ''You're awfully respectful of Mackie all of a sudden. I don't like ambushes, Gordon. Has something happened between you two that I'm not privy to?''

''Of course nothing has happened,'' Gordon said, a bit too hastily. Nothing *had*. Not really. ''I'm just saying we shouldn't be overconfident. And I want this matter over with for once and for all. No ambushes, no confrontation…just cooperation and closure.''

A tap sounded on the door. Sonia answered, ''Come in.'' It was Mackie.

''I was told to come on back. I hope—'' She stopped abruptly, noticing Gordon. ''I thought this was going to be between you and me,'' she chided Sonia. ''You didn't mention anything about having our clients here.''

''Don't blame Sonia—this was my idea,'' Gordon answered. ''When she called and told me of your meeting, I invited myself.''

Sonia nodded, verifying Gordon's explanation of his presence.

''I feel a bit ganged-up on,'' Mackie said rebukingly. Not that she didn't think she could hold her own, but she *was* aggravated.

''We don't plan to do that,'' Gordon drawled. ''Actually I hope the negotiations will remain amiable.''

"I'll do *my* part," Mackie answered, giving him a condescending smile.

"So will I," Gordon answered, knowing he was overstepping himself by taking charge, but unable to stop. "Let's get one item clarified from the beginning though. I'm willing to bargain...only Beth isn't about to be in a position of control over Ashley this coming weekend, or ever again. Is that clear?"

"Is that what this is about, Mr. Galloway? Wresting control from Beth? I thought it was about what was best for Ashley."

"In my book that *is* what's best for Ashley."

"How about some coffee for everyone," Sonia chirped, turning to the credenza and bringing a carafe and stack of cups over.

The woman speaks. The way Galloway was running the show, Mackie was beginning to question whether Sonia was suffering from a bout of laryngitis. "Thank you." Mackie accepted the coffee.

"I've done my best to explain Beth's unfortunate circumstances to Mr. Galloway," she said to Sonia, "why she couldn't spend as much time with Ashley as she wanted. Surely the two of you will agree, I've gone the extra mile to accommodate everyone's needs. And then to receive that petition...out of the blue without so much—"

"Sonia and I both called, tried to talk to you, to tell you the petition was coming," Gordon interjected.

"Oh, yes. Sonia phoned less than an hour before the courier arrived and since I wasn't in we didn't talk. And before I heard from you, the petition was already in my hands.''

"That wasn't what we planned. You'd have heard from us first if the delivery service hadn't been so darned efficient. Nevertheless, you can't convince me this 'came out of the blue.' Did you really assume I'd roll over and play dead after that first hearing? I *told* you I wouldn't. Then you and Beth handed me the ammunition I needed and I took advantage of it. Not to hurt you…'' He hesitated a second, hoping Mackie could understand that. "Or even to hurt Beth. But admit it, in my place, you'd have done the same thing. Did you expect any less of me?''

"Yes…no,'' Mackie answered, pressing her fingers hard against the arms of her chair, drawing the blood from her fingertips, making them as white as the hot anger inside her. Anger at Gordon and at herself for being drawn to him even now. "I expected some honor from you,'' she managed to reply.

"I suppose honor is another of those things that's in the eye of the beholder. To me, defending my daughter, protecting her, *is* honorable.'' Gordon could feel his temperature soaring. He was trying to play nice here. Why did Mackie have to be so unyielding?

"I don't disagree with your need to protect your daughter. You get a Good Daddy Medal for that. What I need is for you to take off the blinders and see other positions besides your own.''

She shot a glare at Sonia Mott who was leaning back in her chair listening to the byplay. A little help from the woman wouldn't be amiss, but Sonia seemed content just to sit there and let her client do all the talking. Nice way to earn your fee.

Mackie took a deep breath and started again. "I'm not so foolish as to believe what happened with Beth won't give Judge Fillmore pause," Mackie said calmly, "and believe me, I want to do the right thing. However—"

"Spare me," Gordon interrupted. "A lawyer with scruples." He rolled his eyes to the ceiling, then quickly sought Mackie's again.

Without saying a word, Mackie glanced pointedly at Sonia.

"I'm sorry, Sonia," Gordon apologized, realizing he'd insulted his own attorney along with Mackie. "That was out of line."

"You're just upset," Sonia soothed, "I understand how frustrating this is."

That's a good one. Let your rich client degrade our profession, then give him a consoling pat on the back. Sonia's deference to Gordon made Mackie wonder if the woman's interest in him went beyond the professional. Immediately Mackie felt contrite for the catty thought. After all, *her* interests wouldn't exactly pass any standard of purity and to disparage Sonia was a perfect example of the pot calling the kettle black.

Another deep breath from Mackie as she tried to get back on the subject. "Sonia's right, this is frustrating. Frustrating for all concerned. So why don't we try to figure out a solution? I'm sure we'd all prefer to find one ourselves rather than having a judge impose his own."

"I already have a solution," Gordon volunteered.

"Oh, yes, the old 'all or nothing at all' solution. Well, Mr. Galloway, Beth's position may be somewhat weakened, but just like you, she's not going to 'roll over and play dead.' Denying her all access to her daughter simply because that's the way you want things won't cut it with Beth."

"I believe it will if I offer enough money."

"She's already turned you down once."

"Only because the bounty wasn't high enough."

"You're singing the same old song."

"And you're not listening. As much as it chafes me to reward extortion, that's what I'm prepared to do here. But I don't intend to set off a feeding frenzy. I know Beth. She can run through money faster than water through a sieve. I'll be fair, but I won't be a cash machine for the rest of my life." He massaged his temples.

"Just because you think it to be true, we still don't know that money is Beth's motive."

"You're her attorney. It's your job to find out."

"I'm well aware of my job, Mr. Galloway."

"Fine. Then here's what I propose. A check for fifty thousand in your hands as soon as Beth signs on the dotted line...no better make that one hundred thousand. Beth is greedy.

"Tell Beth I'll pay her a hundred grand to drop the custody suit, get out of our lives—and stay out. It should be an appealing amount to her. Oh, you might also tell my former wife the ante's not going any higher. This is a take it or leave it offer."

"An offer that's unfair to both Beth *and* Ashley. Haven't you heard—most children have an innate need to be with their mothers. Do you feel justified in making such a momentous decision for Ashley— to exile her mother from her life?"

"Damn right I do!" Gordon slammed his fist on the table to emphasize his point. "When her safety is in question, there's no end to the decisions I'll take responsibility for."

"The judge has already addressed the safety issue and dismissed it."

"That was before. Beth has thoughtfully provided fresh grist for the mill with her cavalier attitude toward Ashley."

Mackie twisted her earring. *True enough.* Beth had been willing to dump her child into the lap of the handiest person without any thought to Ashley. Sonia could make something of that. But Mackie still had to try to secure a better arrangement. For everyone, she hoped—but especially for Ashley and Beth. Beth could use the money, sure, but there was so much more to these negotiations than mere numbers with dollar signs in front of them.

"I can't agree with what you're proposing," Mackie said. "Even putting aside the obvious—that Ashley may want to get to know her mother one day—there are many other considerations. What about possible medical consequences? In later years, Ashley may need some answers. For instance, whether there's a genetic connection to diabetes or heart trouble. And there's family heritage to think of, too. Her roots. Most people want to know where they came from, about their ancestors. Which grandparent had the same hair color, body build, temperament.''

''I can tell her most of those things. Beth isn't a phantom, an unknown. She's simply a bad mother.''

''Here we go again,'' Mackie said in an exasperated voice. Gordon wasn't about to acknowledge any point of view except his own.

''And we'll keep going until I make you understand.''

''It seems to me you're the one who's not understanding.''

''Please, can we just stick to facts and eliminate the critical commentary?'' Sonia interjected.

''Thank you,'' Mackie said, relieved the woman was finally coming through. About time.

''Mackie, how would you like another cup of coffee in my office while Gordon and I take a few minutes to consult?''

''That sounds like the best idea I've heard since I arrived.'' She rose from her chair. ''Call me when you're through.''

Ten minutes later, a secretary summoned Mackie back from Sonia's office to the conference room.

''OK, OK,'' Gordon said, before she could open her mouth. ''How about this?—in exchange for a financial settlement, Beth gives me sole custody and I give my word she can have limited visitation.''

''Your word?'' Mackie gave him a stare of disbelief. ''Oh sure, I can see it now. Beth signs away her parental claims, then you renege on the offer. Wasn't it a Hollywood director who said 'An oral contract isn't worth the paper it's written on'? Beth would be left with nothing but your word."

"*And my money.* As far as my word goes, though, you may have no faith in that, but Beth knows I don't go back on promises. I *will* let her see Ashley. Although, to be honest, I doubt that she'll avail herself of the opportunity very often—if ever."

"I don't like it," Mackie answered. "And neither will Beth."

"Like it or not, it's this or another go-round with Judge Fillmore. So why don't you quit being Miss High-and-mighty and just ask Beth whether she likes it or not. It's really her decision, not yours."

Mackie fumed at the reprimand. She resented being treated as if she didn't have the brains of a potted plant. Sonia, who was getting the same treatment, should object, too. "Why do you even bother with legal representation, Mr. Galloway, since you fly solo most of the time?" Mackie frowned at her colleague. "Haven't you got anything to say, Sonia?"

"At Alexander, Mott and Percy, we strive to please the client. This is what Mr. Galloway wants."

"OK, if you insist. As you've so graciously reminded me—" she threw a glare Gordon's way "—it's Beth's decision, not mine. I'll talk with her this afternoon. But don't hold your breath that you're going to get your way on this."

Mackie phoned Beth the second she reached her office. Beth wasn't home. When she finally returned

Mackie's call in late afternoon, she was at work and couldn't talk. They scheduled an appointment first thing Tuesday.

Once Mackie had laid out Gordon's proposal, Beth sat with fingers peaked in front of her. "One hundred K? No sirree. It's not nearly enough."

Mackie was aghast. She'd expected Beth to be affronted over Gordon's offer that she be totally cut off from custody. No, not merely affronted, absolutely furious. Instead Beth's only quarrel seemed to be over the amount. In other words, in Beth's eyes Ashley was for sale.

Suddenly all remaining fight drained out of Mackie. She'd hung in long enough. Maybe too long. Gordon had been right when he'd insisted money was the issue. Beth had duped her, played her like a fiddle. Mackie felt like the biggest fool ever.

"And Ashley? What about her?" she asked Beth, her emotions barely under control.

Beth appeared unperturbed by the accusatory tone in Mackie's voice. "You've seen Gordon with her. No man is a better father. Why, he bonded with Ashley from the instant they first let him hold her. It was enough to make a woman jealous the way he carried on."

Mackie shook her head in wonderment but Beth maintained her insouciant demeanor.

"So you're willing to take the money and just walk away?"

Beth gave a half smile. "Sorry to disappoint you,

Mackie, but despite your fairy-tale ideas about motherhood, I'm not cut out for the position.''

Fairy-tale ideas? If Mackie was certain about only one thing, it was that all her ideas about motherhood were sensible, earthbound. Beth was the one living in fantasyland, not she. "Tell me...your having to work and the car trouble...was it all a lie?"

"Not all of it. Maybe I could have gotten out of work if I'd absolutely had to, though. And my car did act up, but I could have had it fixed much quicker...especially if I'd had the cash to go to a regular garage instead of a guy working in his backyard.'' She gestured around Mackie's luxurious office. "You don't know how it is living hand-to-mouth."

For a moment Mackie felt called to task—as if Beth were suggesting that these nice surroundings got in the way of Mackie's ability to be empathetic. Then she got herself in check. She couldn't let Beth's off-putting behavior get in the way of the practical advice she was supposed to be providing.

"Maybe I'm not living hand-to-mouth as you've implied, but that doesn't prevent me from coming up with another way to solve your situation. Like requesting assistance from your ex-husband until you get on your feet.''

Beth fairly curled her lip. "If I asked for something monthly, it would take years to come up even to the hundred grand he's offering. I need more—now."

"Then *the money* is enough for you?" Try as she might, Mackie couldn't keep the ice from her tone.

The idea was repugnant to her. Still, she had to remember her role here. Not to play moral flame keeper, but to help her client get what she desired. "Are you sure that down the line you're not going to regret being separated from Ashley." She had to make one last-ditch effort.

"Gordon said I could see her. He wouldn't let me before so that's a plus. And I don't *want* the day-to-day responsibility, Mackie. Never did. As long as I get the dollars I'm entitled to, I will be satisfied."

Mackie thought of all the women longing to have a child and here sat one who considered her offspring nothing but a bargaining tool. *How dare Beth do this?* Ashley was a handful, but she was also lovable...for the most part, a darling.

"And what do you consider you're 'entitled to'?" Mackie asked stonily.

"A million dollars has a nice ring to it. Gordon inherited over fifty million...he won't even miss it."

Mackie's disgust surged. Before, she had not known the full extent of Gordon's inheritance. Still, even if his aunt's legacy comprised the entire gold reserves at Fort Knox, Beth didn't deserve a penny. It was exactly as Gordon had said—extortion. Pure and simple.

"Afford it or not, I can't see me asking for that with a straight face."

"Because your sympathies are now with Gordon?" Beth cocked her head suspiciously.

"My sympathies have nothing to do with it,"

Mackie replied sharply. "It's the amount that's ludicrous. I don't care to appear ridiculous."

"Neither do I," Beth retorted. "If Gordon and I were still married, I'd be entitled to half his fortune. A million is a mere pittance and—"

"But you're not *still* married," Mackie broke in. "And even if you were, the inheritance would be Gordon's separate property. You have *no* entitlements."

"The way you're rooting for Gordon, I'm beginning to wonder whether my lawyer has been swayed by Gordon's blue eyes and compromised—"

"I've done no such thing," Mackie blurted, smoke threatening to pour from her ears. She didn't know when she'd felt so incensed. Beth's accusation was outrageous, simply outrageous. Mackie hadn't been swayed by those Galloway eyes. Not one bit. Not that she didn't find them dangerously compelling. But it would take a lot more than a pair of eyes to make her scrap her allegiance to a client.

"If you feel that way, you're free to go to someone else. We have no binding contract."

"Now, Mackie, I didn't mean to hurt your feelings."

That syrupy little-girl tone Beth sometimes used made Mackie want to scream. She had half a notion to insist Beth buzz off, find another lawyer to chase after the big bucks. Then again, why prolong the inevitable? Bringing matters to a conclusion was the way to go. Especially for Ashley.

Even if she was supposed to be Beth's advocate,

Mackie knew the best thing for Ashley probably *was* a total break from this poor excuse for a parent. Could an indifferent, money-grubbing mother like Beth offer anything but heartache for the little girl?

But what about Gordon? A million dollars? She could imagine the blistering her ears would take after telling him that. Would he part with so much? Not likely. He'd said his last offer was the final one.

Mackie placed a phone call to Sonia, who had the same "get real" reaction as Mackie, but agreed to relay what had happened. She dialed back within minutes, shock in her voice. It was a done deal.

Straightening up in her chair, Mackie sat stunned. Gordon had gone along with the million. Now as she thought about it, however, she should have known he would. He'd have forked over any amount of money to secure Ashley's future. Unlike Beth, it was his daughter that mattered most to him. He'd agreed to his ex-wife's over-the-top request, probably thinking he was coming out ahead in the bargain.

"You're getting what you requested," she told Beth.

"Yes!" shouted Beth, pumping a fist.

"I'll draw up some papers and get them over to Sonia for review. Once the agreement's completed, your signature will be needed."

"Give me a call and I'll speed right over." Beth stopped at the door. "You know...we probably should have asked for *two* million."

It took all of Mackie's strength not to sling her glass paperweight at the door closing behind Beth.

*   *   *

Mackie and Sonia worked out the wording, then later that day, Beth came in to sign the necessary papers. Mackie intended to hand-carry them to Sonia's on her way home. "It's all over," she sighed. No more arguments, no more Ashley, no more Gordon. She felt empty.

She was packing her briefcase to leave when her secretary advised that Gordon Galloway was there to see her. Mackie inhaled deeply, taking a moment to compose herself. I stand corrected, she told herself, it's all over but the shouting.

No doubt Gordon wanted to take her to task one last time before he vacated her life. But then again, since her hands felt dirtied from the huge settlement she secured for Beth, she supposed she deserved his contempt.

The sky was wintry, a few snowflakes mixed with rain. Old Man Winter having a rare final hurrah in February, adding to Mackie's somber mood. She sighed and walked to the door to invite Gordon in.

In his arms was Ashley, clutching a small doll. "Hi," the little girl said, obviously recognizing Mackie from their time together.

"Hello, Ashley," Mackie answered, surprised he'd brought her along.

Gordon strolled over to Mackie's desk and lay down a bank draft. She picked up the draft and ran her fingers over a number one followed by six zeros. It looked fake—like one of those misleading sweepstakes checks that come in the mail announcing "You Mackie Smith are a winner."

Mackie could feel the muscles in her neck tighten just from holding the check. "You didn't have to bring this personally."

"I know." His eyes moved slowly around her office, giving it the scrutiny of a newly hired interior decorator. "Expensive but not ostentatious. Neat and organized. It suits you."

Although Gordon had been to the firm once before, when he'd brought Ashley that first Friday night, they'd met in the conference room. Somehow, being here together in the confines of her small space seemed too close to Mackie, too intimate.

"Glad you approve," she said coolly, determined to get control of her wits. She looked down at the check again. "It's a lot of money."

"Money well spent."

He was being altogether too nice. Mackie couldn't detect whether it was merely the eye of the storm, or if, now that things were truly over, Gordon was turning loose of his animosity. Nonetheless, his lack of malice made her feel even more sullied.

"You were right and I was wrong," Mackie said. "Beth..." She stopped herself and shook her head vigorously. "Forget I said that. It was unprofessional."

He waved a hand of dismissal. "What does it matter now? Quit chewing on the rights and wrongs and accept that you can't be all-knowing every minute." Sitting down in the wing chair beside her desk, he balanced Ashley on his knee. "The money means nothing to me except the fact it brought down the curtain on this farce. Having that suit hanging over my head was getting to me. I'm grateful you persuaded Beth.''

"Persuaded? Don't give me any credit. That's the last thing I want.''

"No, I don't believe you do." He heaved a deep breath. "Do you have some papers for me to sign? Or have they been sent to Sonia?''

"I was going to take them over.''

"Then I've saved you a trip.''

"Sonia might prefer you wait until she sees the final product.''

"You've worked it out together. Don't worry about Sonia.''

Mackie sat down in her swivel chair and passed a sheaf of documents across to him. Gordon read the first page and was turning to the second when Ashley pulled on the agreement, threatening to tear it. Gordon shifted her in his arms.

"Here, let me take her," Mackie offered, standing up to get Ashley and carrying her over to the window. It was snowing harder now. "Look, Ashley." Mackie searched her memory, then came up with a song from her childhood about a dancing snowflake.

Gordon shifted his attention from the documents to the window, finding himself mesmerized by the sight of this impeccable woman—today in a dark brown suit and a lighter beige blouse. Once, he would have considered the outfit, along with the woman, austere. Now he noticed a softness about it, the clinginess of the blouse, the way the skirt molded her hips as

Mackie tapped on the window and crooned to his daughter.

There was a softness about Mackie, too. She and Ashley seemed so natural together. *But there's nothing natural about it,* Gordon reminded himself, redirecting his attention to the documents. Mackie Smith was a career woman extraordinaire—not the mommy sort at all. And the role she'd played in upsetting their lives…well, that was just plain awful.

He shouldn't have come here, should have let Sonia handle these details the way she'd wanted to until he insisted on performing the task himself.

He needed to finish his business, grab Ashley from Mackie Smith's grasp and get out of here. "Everything appears in order," he said, bringing a halt to another of Mackie's snow-themed songs. "Shall I sign now, or do we need a notary?"

"We have someone on staff," Mackie answered, going to her telephone, but still not relinquishing Ashley.

Five minutes later, the notary handed the executed documents to Mackie. All the *i*s were dotted and *t*s crossed. It was truly and irrevocably finished now. Mackie gave Gordon a copy.

"Well, I suppose this is goodbye," he said, coming around her desk to gather up his daughter.

"Yes, I suppose it is," she answered, unaccountably bereft as she surrendered Ashley and watched them leave. It was absolutely irrational how she'd felt when he took Ashley—as if the child was being torn from her arms. "Get a grip," Mackie scolded aloud.

So it was hard to let Ashley go...that was only because she was an appealing child. It had nothing to do with any personal desire of Mackie's to be a mother. Not any more than it had to do with the fact that losing Ashley also meant losing Gordon. Neither of them were ever in the cards for Mackie anyway. She needed to remember that.

CHAPTER SIX

NORMALLY work took up the lion's share of the weekend for Mackie, the remainder filled with chores and occasional outings with dates or girlfriends. But for the next seventy-two hours, she'd cleared her agenda. No work, no household tasks, no social obligations. It was President's Day weekend and she'd promised to indulge herself for the next three days, to refill the pitcher, so to speak.

Saturday morning she'd lazed over the newspaper before heading to the gym. An hour of step aerobics, a soak in the whirlpool, then an appointment to have her hair and nails done. After that a health food shake and a neck massage.

Already Mackie was feeling better, more centered. For the past few months, even before the mess with the Galloways, she'd been restless, not exactly unhappy with her existence, but not satisfied, either. Something had been missing—exactly what, unclear.

Rather than confessing that the "something missing" was no longer quite so ambiguous, that the hours spent with Gordon and Ashley had begun to define what was absent, Mackie preferred to rationalize.

"I've gotten in a rut, that's all," she said aloud as her fingers did a tattoo on the car's steering wheel while she waited for the light to change. It was the career gal syndrome. Nothing more. Work late, plop in front of the TV with a frozen dinner, go to bed too tired to read even the mail.

The afternoon's itinerary might not have much pizzazz, but at least it should cure the weariness. She was going to head home, slip into a bathrobe, turn off the telephone ringer, then read and lounge around with no interruptions. There was even a box of fudge in her nightstand she could dip into. Pure indulgence.

But first a stop at Book Emporium. She needed something more entertaining than a law journal to escape from reality with.

Mackie roamed the aisles, selecting a spy thriller and a romance and was debating whether to overload herself with a recent bestseller set in Spain. She reached for the book at the same time a male voice behind her said, "I understand it's a good read."

Mackie glanced up at a pair of now-familiar blue eyes. Gordon Galloway. And next to him a sleeping Ashley in her stroller, her palm curved around a chubby cheek. Mackie had to stem the urge to touch the child…to touch the father too. She had expected never to see them again.

"If I didn't know better, I'd say you were following me," she whispered to Gordon, using banter to control her excitement. In just an instant her heartbeat had accelerated and a flustered state come over her.

The feelings disturbed Mackie, especially since she couldn't figure out why she was letting him affect her like this. Until meeting Gordon, Mackie had never been one of those women who allowed a man's physical features to influence her one way or the other.

Well, so much for her carefree day of total relaxation. Just seeing Gordon had tautened every muscle in her body, sent every emotion racing into overdrive.

And it wasn't only Gordon who stirred up emotions, but Ashley as well. Mackie's heart had done a pitty-pat when she saw that baby too. It was not the same as with Gordon naturally, but nonetheless disquieting.

"Following you? Right," he said. "I bring my daughter along as a decoy while I prey on unsuspecting females. My speciality is bookstores."

"Must be an expensive criminal outlet." She gestured to Gordon's own stack of books stowed in the pouch of Ashley's stroller. "Do you prey in the fiction or nonfiction section?"

"Actually both…don't want to limit myself." He grinned, a swell of relief inside him that Mackie seemed to harbor no bitterness over the way he'd handled the Beth thing—rushing in with the new motion, dominating the discussions with her and Sonia…

Even though he'd told himself that he had no cause for remorse over his activities, he'd had it anyway. Standing here and joking with her lightened those feelings.

"By the way I was serious about this one." He added the selection to his pile.

"OK, I'll take your advice." She grabbed a copy too. "At the gallery you mentioned your writing. Is anything of yours on the shelves here?"

"In my dreams. So far, I've published one book and the only way I could get it inside this place would be to smuggle it in or to buy the store. Hey, maybe that's an idea. I've been looking for companies to invest my money in."

"Your book's not mainstream then?"

He laughed. "You might say that. There isn't a big clamor among the general public for a treatise on World War II battle strategies."

"Too bad," she said consolingly. "Tell you what. I'll buy a copy and talk it up. What's the title, by the way?"

"Actually that *was* the title... *World War II Battle Strategies*. Not a grabber, huh?"

Mackie tried not to laugh. "No, I can't picture it on any bestseller lists. You should have called it something more provocative. Obviously you don't watch enough daytime television or you'd have chosen something like *Battle Strategies of the Sexes*."

He rubbed his jaw. "Great idea, only there's a tiny flaw with that notion—my book has absolutely nothing to do with sex."

"Well, there you have it. Now you know where you went wrong. You'll just have to correct that oversight in your future writing. Think mass market."

She gave a teasing laugh and Gordon smiled in response. Since the meeting in her office Tuesday he'd given a lot of thought to Mackie. The image of her with Ashley in her arms...the image of Mackie in *his* arms. It had been a long time since he'd let a woman get under his skin.

Heck, after Beth had finished working him over, he'd wondered if a vow of chastity could be so bad. Now, with Mackie this close, her complexion all pink and dewy and looking as baby soft as Ash's, he suddenly couldn't think of anything much worse.

"Excuse me, sir, ma'am. Would you please clear the aisle for a second?" A clerk with a trolley of magazines was trying to push past them.

"Sorry," Mackie said, easing out of the way.

"That must be our cue to quit loitering and start buying," he said, pushing the baby stroller into the next aisle. "Well...see you."

"Yeah, see you." She bent down to speak to Ashley, but the little girl was still asleep, a tiny milk bubble between her lips. Now that was the kind of "What, me worry?" approach to life she needed. To be able to tune out like that. Too bad children were the only ones capable of taking their ease anywhere and everywhere. "I'd say goodbye to Ashley, but she seems dead to the world."

"Looks that way," Gordon agreed. Intending to get a book or two for Ashley, he tarried behind as Mackie started toward the checkout counter. He snatched up a book about puppies, then immediately replaced it on the shelves. He was having a difficult time concentrating on preschool stories as he watched Mackie in line at the cashier's desk. She was reading the flyleaf on one of her purchases, oblivious to the fact that he was studying her.

How was it that she continued to push all his buttons? It had begun while his defenses were down, when he was torn up over his and Ashley's plight. Then some time during those hours when Mackie had been part of their daily existence, she'd flipped a switch that had activated his hormones. And for the life of him, he couldn't seem to find an Off switch. Didn't even want to anymore.

His early hostility toward her had long since transformed into something else entirely. Whenever Mackie was around, the air fairly vibrated with electricity. Gordon's body stirred at the thought of her, enveloping her in his arms, running his fingers through her lustrous hair, pressing his lips against hers. Mackie Smith was the most kissable woman he'd ever locked lips with. He could just imagine— *you're imagining way too much already, fella,* he cautioned, noticing Mackie coming back toward him.

She smiled. "I forgot to ask—where does one go to buy your book? Street peddlers? Book pushers?"

"Nothing so colorful. Try the university bookstore."

"OK, I will. Bye."

"Bye," he said, and watched her walk off for the second time.

Wearing silk pajamas, Mackie lay in bed taking in the ten o'clock news, when her telephone rang. She turned down the television volume and reached for the receiver.

"Mackie? Gordon. Sorry to call on a Saturday night like this..." He paused. "I know it's late..."

"That's OK," she said. Her heartbeat jumped to

aerobic workout level. "Is anything wrong? Is it Beth?"

"Beth? Oh, no, nothing like that." His answer was slow in coming as if he were trying to remember: Beth? Beth who?

"After our conversation about my book today," he began, "I started thinking—'if she's game enough to read the thing, the least you can do is get her a copy.' So I was wondering if you'd like to go to breakfast tomorrow morning and I'll present you with one— autographed if you like."

Mackie was grateful for her courtroom experience, which enabled her to speak when she was numb— like now. He was actually asking her to go to breakfast with him? "Breakfast?"

"You know—that morning meal a lot of people eat."

Mackie leaned back against her pillow. This invitation sounded suspiciously like a date. Not an accidental meeting, not a business meeting, not being thrown together by circumstances, but a *real* date. A few weeks ago, she'd have sooner expected to hear Dallas footballer Troy Aikman inviting her for a meal. Or even Monaco's Prince Albert. Anyone but Gordon Galloway.

Mackie's mind ran through a checklist. If she said yes, she would be willingly going out with a recent courtroom opponent. Not something advocated in law school. And not the most politic move for a young attorney who believed in walking the straight and narrow.

Was it legal? Yes. Ethical?—sorta. Controversial? Absolutely, possibly even giving the impression of having gone over to the other side. But she hadn't. She'd remained steadfast to her nightmare of a client to the very end and gotten her just what she wanted. Mackie no longer represented Beth and owed her no further loyalty.

And she really wanted to see Gordon again. Something was going on here, something that piqued her curiosity. Common sense said she was no more Gordon Galloway's type of woman than he was her type of man, but the whys of the pursuit intrigued her. Surely he wasn't *that* desperate for someone to read his book.

Curiosity won out over how this would look. "I suppose I could eke out some time for breakfast. Since I have to eat anyway..." She allowed the sentence to trail off.

"Very flattering, Ms. Smith. I usually don't have to beg women to dine with me."

"Women, huh? And would that mean lots?" As a single father, Gordon obviously didn't have much opportunity for the playboy routine. And he'd told her that he'd cooled it, as he put it, with the opposite sex. But he could have been playing it safe in front of Beth's lawyer. For all Mackie knew, there could be a revolving door of women coming to his home, wanting to do their bit for the poor lonely male.

Gordon hated to admit that, no, there weren't lots of women, that—when it came right down to it—

there weren't any. He hedged. "Which Mackie Smith wants to know? The woman or the attorney?"

He could almost hear her snarl over the phone.

"I refuse to have breakfast with you if you're going to be suspicious of my every word," she countered. "The case is over, remember?"

He smiled. It was so easy to pull her chain. And fun. Mackie added a new facet to his life. Spirited and feisty, she made him feel alive. "I'll be on my best behavior," he promised. "Shall I pick you up at nine-thirty?"

By ten on Sunday they were seated across from each other at a table at S&S Restaurant. Gordon still couldn't believe he had actually asked her out. Last night he'd been going through old letters and journals, getting background for a lecture, when it dawned on him that he didn't want to work all weekend. He'd retrieved Mackie's number and, without stopping to think it through, called.

Afterward he'd had regrets, admonishing himself for acting rashly. Now those regrets had dissipated and he was enjoying the view across the table. The hair shiny as a shampoo ad, that smooth touchable skin and those full Cupid's bow lips, which lately seemed so sensuous.

He'd be a liar not to own up to the fact that he was smitten. Such a waste. Why did Mackie Smith have to be the polar opposite of what he needed in a woman?

But, hey buddy, you haven't asked her here to propose. You're just getting out, testing the dating waters again. Besides, he could do much worse finding someone to spend a few hours with. Mackie was attractive and intelligent, never tiresome. Even when they were fighting, she was fascinating. Fascinating, but always a challenging companion.

If he ever took the marriage plunge again, however, it would be with someone whose first priority was home and family, someone who could share his devotion to Ashley. From all he'd seen of Mackie, she was consumed with career.

When he met her gaze, he realized she was studying him, those lips he'd been admiring now wearing a slight smile.

"Something funny?"

"Looks like I caught you in some heavy concentration," she said.

"Sorry. Didn't mean to zone out on you." He returned her smile. "Two weeks ago if someone had forecast I'd be here with you, I'd have accused them of insanity."

"So who's ready for the funny farm—you or the forecasters?" She ruffled her brow.

"Neither," he said. "Although you'll have to admit it's pretty unusual…going at it tooth and nail in litigation…then going out with each other. Not your usual pickup situation."

"Well, don't forget, we've spent a lot of time together outside of court."

"I realize that all too well. And you know what? I'm glad. Ms. Smith, you've started growing on me."

"Like a fungus you mean?"

"Definitely not like a fungus. You're a hard lady to compliment. Can it be so difficult to believe I like your company and let it go at that?"

"It just seems so improbable coming from you."

"Well, I do like your company. And while I'm tossing out kudos, you're not bad to look at, either." *Damn beautiful in my estimation.*

She rearranged the silverware on the table in front of her, unaccountably shy. "Quite flattering coming from a catch like you…moderately attractive, somewhat entertaining…" Mackie aimed for flippancy to cover her unease. "Not the sort of guy to be fancy-free on a long holiday weekend."

"Well, this is unusual. I'm seldom fancy-free. Although the lady who takes up most of my time is just past her first birthday."

"Where is Ashley anyway?" Mackie asked.

"My mother has her for a couple of days. Picked her up last night and I've been wringing my hands ever since." Gordon shook his head ruefully. "Knew I would feel that way, but she's been hounding me to let Ash stay over at her house and I finally relented. Except for her nanny days, I don't leave Ash much in the care of others." His jaw tightened. "So you can see how the Beth thing really hit me from all sides, almost made me crazy."

"We're not going to get into anything, are we?" Mackie chided. "End up in a fight—throwing food, utensils…knives?"

"No, I made a promise to be on my best behavior

and I'm keeping it. You're safe." He smiled, then placed his hand on hers.

Uncomfortable with the awareness his touch generated, Mackie pulled her hand away and rested it in her lap. "So how is it? Having Ashley gone for the weekend?"

"Strange. Like I left an arm somewhere. It's going to be a long time before Mom talks me into letting her go like this again. Still it gave me an opportunity to get out and about."

"I don't know what I think about being a stand-in for a fifteen-month-old," Mackie said teasingly.

"Don't worry." Elbows on the table, he leaned toward her. "My thoughts of you aren't the least bit fatherly."

Mackie took a breath. She was teasing, he was teasing, still... He'd promised her safety—she didn't feel one bit safe. Too much dangerous chemistry. This conversation needed redirection. "Have you started any of the new books you bought?"

"Finished one last night."

"Tell me about it."

For the next hour and a half they sat at the restaurant, discussing first popular fiction, then a smattering of this and that, slowly learning more about each other. A hovering waitress and the line forming at the restaurant's entrance eventually prompted Mackie to comment—albeit reluctantly, "I think we've overstayed our allotted table time."

"Then we'd better scram." He checked the tab,

fished some bills from his wallet and placed them on the table.

Gordon was walking Mackie to the car when he took her arm and paused. "Look, you told me you enjoy movies and there's a film at the Inwood by a new Swedish director I've heard good things about. The first show's at one. How about giving it a try?"

Mackie hesitated. The sensible answer was to refuse, cut this off before she got in any deeper than she already was. But she didn't want to be sensible. Sensible was highly overrated anyway. "Sure, why not?" She glanced at her watch. Twelve-fifteen. "We can browse and window-shop until then."

After the first film, they exited the theater, bought tickets out front for another, then reentered the lobby. Mackie hadn't seen a double feature since she was a teenager. Nor had she done anything frivolous in months. She felt youthful, carefree, like a butterfly let loose in a field of wildflowers.

When they exited the theater a second time, it was nearing six. Gordon suggested dinner. After some give and take, they agreed on Italian food, deciding on a restaurant neither had tried.

"I haven't been here before, but I love pasta…all kinds," Mackie said.

"Me, too. We've found a lot of things we have in common today."

And avoided focusing on the things we don't. But the day had been too pleasurable to ruin it by dwelling on such practicalities. She had committed herself to a few hours of escape and had no intention of scrapping her plan now. For the rest of the evening, she was simply going to enjoy herself.

How the conversation veered from the get-acquainted mode to the very personal, Mackie wasn't certain. It had begun when they talked about her work, about her entrance into family law. "My first case involved a mother who was trying to keep her kids away from a tyrannical ex-husband. In retaliation, he absconded with their two children during a routine visitation. The mother has frantically searched for her children, but they have yet to be found. I ache for that woman, the way—"

Mackie stopped in midsentence and sighed. She thought of Gordon's determination that Beth be barred from Ashley's life, glad she'd been able to persuade him to change his mind on the issue. "A child should be able to have access to both parents. Your daughter included."

The words had bubbled out before she could block the flow and Mackie immediately reproached herself for saying too much. She didn't want to pick a fight with Gordon tonight. Things were going so well and wasn't that what she'd charged him with earlier? Picking a fight.

"You won that argument, remember," he said, apparently not offended. "My preference would be for Beth to be out of Ash's life forever, but I don't want my daughter to hate me later on, to think that somehow I was responsible for her mother's absence. That's the only reason I agreed that Beth can see Ashley if she wants to. And, as I said before, I'll be surprised if she ever takes advantage of the privilege. She got what she wanted and my guess is that she's quit her job and left town.''

Mackie nodded. Beth had done exactly that. So much for her client's reformation into a model of stability. ''She's quit her job and gone off to lead the good life. In Mexico, I think.'' Telling him that news wasn't violating any attorney-client privilege and it probably increased his level of security.

''Great. I wish her a long, happy stay. Now how about getting off this subject.''

''Sounds like a good idea.''

''Tell you what, let's follow a completely different tack. Did you notice the restaurant has a fortune-teller in the lounge?''

She eyed him askance. ''You're suggesting we get our fortunes told?''

''Just for fun, what do you say?''

Pausing for a second, Mackie finally said, ''OK, why not?'' One more chance today for going with the flow.

The fortune-teller was an older woman—late sixties—and dressed rather staidly for her profession. No formulaic bandanna and hoop earrings, but a simple black sheath, her only concession to jewelry, a clunky gold bracelet.

Mackie went first, Gordon having decided on a brandy in the bar. The woman took her hand and studied it, then began talking while Mackie assumed a sincere expression as if she believed in this tomfoolery. But the woman's words made Mackie swallow her skepticism, or at least wonder if she'd been set up. No, it couldn't be. Still she was relieved Gordon was out of earshot rather than by her side listening to the predictions.

"I can glimpse sorrow in your past. A man... someone close to you...your husband perhaps. There is pain. But the future holds only happiness. A new man has entered your life...a good man. You must forget your fears and trust him. He is your future. I see a wedding...a child...great love."

Mackie was shocked, though still wary. *This is coincidence. Mere coincidence.* The woman probably had a whole set of stock phrases. "You'll find happiness, you'll take a trip to an exotic place...you'll win a prize, yada, yada, yada." But her words were hitting too close to home, especially the sorrow in the past part.

Then again, a wedding in Mackie's immediate future? Hardly. And the new man, Gordon? Guess again, lady. The seer had sized up the dynamics of Gordon and Mackie as a couple and leaped to conclusions—all erroneous.

It wasn't that Mackie was phobic about marriage. Even though she'd had her own sorry excuse of a union—and heard about hundreds of other star-crossed couplings in her practice—she knew happy-ever-afters did exist.

Her parents were a living testament to that fact, and adamant that love waited just around the corner for their daughter. Her mother constantly quizzed her on whether Mr. Wonderful had come into her life yet.

Wouldn't Mom just beam if she could hear what the fortune-teller was saying about her daughter's marital prospects? Well, Mackie didn't plan on sharing that little tidbit. Mom would start poring through brides' magazines and compiling guest lists.

Fifteen minutes later Mackie was sipping a Brandy Alexander and gazing over at the table where Gordon had taken his turn with the psychic. He had a pensive look on his face as he listened. Was he being fed the same love and happiness spiel? Probably some silly version of it.

On the drive home, he recounted some of what he'd been told. "She said I'd recently met a woman who needed a loving family as much as I do. Know anyone like that?"

"Not personally," Mackie said, cutting off that line of conversation.

"So what did our clairvoyant tell you?"

"To be a woman of mystery, to reveal nothing," Mackie fibbed.

"Good advice. Men adore women of mystery."

"Then I better do my best to continue the secrecy."

He left her at her front door with a goodbye kiss on the cheek. Mackie went inside and leaned her forehead against the closed door. A hand went up to stroke the cheek he'd kissed as she tried to suppress the realization that she longed for a very different kind of kiss from Gordon Galloway. Get a grip, Mackie admonished herself.

You could say this about the man—he wasn't one

to rush a gal. Though frustrated, Mackie found this old-fashioned reticence endearing. Gordon was an extraordinary man who was going to make some woman a super husband. Only not her. She just hoped he realized that.

CHAPTER SEVEN

DESPITE her intentions to chill out the entire holiday weekend, on Monday morning Mackie was up, dressed and weighing whether or not to go into the office when the telephone rang.

"I had to call and tell you that yesterday was special to me."

"To me, too," she said, instantly recognizing Gordon's voice.

"Mother has insisted on keeping Ash until five. Why don't you come by about noon and I'll fix lunch for us?"

"I'd like that," she said, abandoning all thoughts of work.

"Great. What kind of meal is appropriate for President's Day anyway?"

"I don't think this holiday comes with a meal."

"Then we'll have to start a new tradition. Cherry pie for Washington and, uh, beef for Lincoln."

"Beef?"

"I'm reaching here. Lincoln...Illinois...Chicago stockyards...just go with me."

"You plan it. I'll eat it. See you later."

Gordon greeted her at his door. He was dressed casually in jeans and a plaid flannel shirt. "Welcome," he said, then added, "bet you never imagined when we met a few weeks ago you'd hear that from me someday."

She crossed the threshold and turned his way. "Not unless I thought you were luring me in for foul play."

Demanding to be noticed, Cleo meowed plaintively and did her ankle-circling act and Mackie bent down to scratch the cat's ears.

"Appears you've made a friend," Gordon said, as he led the way to the kitchen, with Mackie and Cleo following behind.

"Something smells good," Mackie said. "What is it?"

"Cherry pie."

She laughed. "You really made one? I thought you were kidding."

"About cherry pie? Never. And I made a roast, too."

"I'm impressed. 'He's good-looking and he cooks.' What more could a girl ask for?" At Gordon's bidding she plopped down onto a tufted leather bar stool at the counter.

"Indeed. Only I have to confess that the pie is from the frozen food aisle."

"And the roast?"

"My own concoction. I put it on to bake before I called you."

"Taking me for granted, huh?"

"No, just hoping for the best. How about a glass of tomato juice for starters?"

"Fine." As Gordon puttered, she sipped her juice

and did an in-depth survey of the room. It was a big country kitchen with hanging copper pots and pans, shelves of cookbooks and a boothed-in eating area. Either Gordon could add decorating to his list of talents or a professional had been involved in putting together a cozy, practical, child-friendly house.

The rooms she'd seen…the hall, the formal living room and the oversize family room adjacent to where she sat, all had shiny hardwood floors and were arranged with durable furniture and fabrics and knickknacks that could take the wear and tear of a little one.

She turned her attention back to her host. Over his jeans Gordon was wearing an apron that said Kiss the Cook and he displayed a natural ease working at the butcher block island. From all appearances, he was really into the cooking scene and this wasn't his first foray into the kitchen.

There's something seductive about a man in an apron, she thought. Maybe it was the appeal of a male in a kitchen—doing something other than getting a beer from the fridge. Then again, maybe it was the appeal of Gordon himself, the blue in his plaid shirt coloring his eyes an even richer shade. *Kissing this particular cook would be a pleasure.* She found it difficult to keep from acting on her thoughts, but managed just to sit still and gawk at him appreciatively.

Gordon cut a glance Mackie's way as he spooned grounds into the coffeemaker. He liked this—a cold February wind shaking the bushes outside. And inside, the kitchen warmed by the central heating and by the oven, the smell of good food enveloping the room.

Most of all, he liked having Mackie here, looking as if she belonged. This wasn't her element of course, she'd admitted kitchens were not her natural habitat. But, nevertheless, casually attired in charcoal slacks and a soft red sweater, her hair pulled back from her face and secured neatly with barrettes, she fitted right into this intimate setting.

"How about a glass of wine with lunch?"

"Sure, but only one. Two at noon will have me rushing home for a nap."

He started to say the obvious, "My bed is yours for the asking," but checked himself. They were edging their way into a nice rapport, and he didn't want to blow it with suggestive remarks. "We can't have that" was his diplomatic reply. The timer buzzed and he grabbed two crocodile-shaped oven mitts to remove the pie from the oven.

"That was delicious," Mackie said, placing her fork onto her plate. The two of them were seated at the booth in front of a large picture window, which gave a sweeping view of the backyard with its swaying live oaks and rippling swimming pool. "But I think I need more coffee. Looking at that pool on a day like today makes me chilly."

"Let's take a second cup to the family room then. I'll get the fireplace going."

As Gordon arranged logs and started a blaze, Mackie studied him. When he joined her on the couch, she'd gotten up the nerve to ask the question she'd been wanting to ask, but had been hesitant about. "Tell me about you and Beth."

Her query seemed to catch him unawares. "I would think you'd be sick and tired of the whole matter. Haven't you heard ten times more than you want to already?"

"Not from you. Do you really prefer me to have only the Beth version? It's rather unflattering and one-sided, you know."

"Undoubtedly, but I figured by now you'd put your own spin on it."

"I have. But I'm still left with a bunch of blanks to be filled. After all, I'm not just a disinterested stranger—I've invested a lot of hours in your marriage...in fact..." She looked away, then looked back, her gaze solemn. "I wish...I'm sorry about what happened."

"Mackie, don't." Gordon reached over and took her hand. "This isn't necessary."

"Yes, it is. I love my job and I rarely feel bad about the cases I'm putting forth. Just the opposite...but this time..."

"...this time," he echoed, "you had a client who didn't deal from the top of the deck."

"That's what I feel rotten about. Like I'm tainted by Beth's mercenary tactics."

"Well you need to remember it was probably inevitable that Beth would come back on the scene with the scent of money in the air. With or without you.

We can thank heaven it worked out fine in the long run."

"You're being generous to me."

"No, I'm not. Beth was the instigator, not you. Like you've told me, you were only doing your job and I want you to know that I've come to understand that. So quit second-guessing yourself. I've finally stopped hating myself over getting involved with her in the first place.

"When a marriage goes wrong, it's difficult not to feel at fault. At the very least, you know you've exercised poor judgment. But despite my regrets, if I hadn't married Beth, I wouldn't have Ashley. And I can't imagine life without my daughter." He shifted his gaze to a clock on the wall. "Speaking of Ash, I'm due to pick her up in an hour."

"Then we'd better start in on those dishes so you won't be late."

"No cleanup for you this time," Gordon said. "I'll tackle the dishes later."

This time. So he planned on there being others. "Well, I'll just be going then. Thanks for the meal." She began walking through the hall toward the front door, Gordon behind her.

"Here, let me help you with your jacket." He held it out for her and as she slid her arms into it, he turned her around to face him. Without a word, he lowered his lips to hers and kissed her. Not a demanding kiss, not a kiss fueled by flames of passion, but simply an exploratory, experimental kind of kiss. He pulled back and looked down into her eyes. "Nice," he drawled.

"Yes," she returned, suddenly very sorry that she had to leave.

"He asked you out and you went?" Taurika's dark eyes widened in astonishment at the latest development in Mackie's Galloway narrative. "Girl, I've heard everything now." Taurika closed Mackie's door and came over to sit by her desk.

"I didn't *plan* on seeing him again. It just happened." Mackie had enjoyed the weekend, but now under Taurika's gaze, she was having a big attack of second thoughts.

"*You* in a relationship with Galloway? That boggles the mind."

"I told you he was attractive. And you were egging me on."

"So what? It's one thing to have a yen for the man—but a real relationship? Girl, I see icebergs ahead."

Mackie waved a dismissive hand. "It's not like that at all."

"Really? Then how is it? You spent the majority of the weekend with the guy. That sounds like a relationship to me. A *troublesome* relationship. The way you met...his having a child. There's some heavy baggage here."

Mackie sighed. What had she been expecting—permission? "Come on, Taurika, it's not as if I intend to marry him." Mackie looked away thoughtfully for a moment. "Even though Gordon Galloway does have a number of qualities any woman would want in a husband."

"Yeah, they're green and they go in a wallet."

"OK, sure most women would appreciate the money."

"Most *men* would appreciate the money. I know a few guys who'd be willing to hook up with him for a stake in fifty mil. It's a lot of loot."

"Yes, it is. But there's so much more. Gordon's sexy, in a rather low-key sort of way, to say nothing of being intelligent and amusing. And I'm beginning to see that he's a pretty nice guy as well. The only thing that seems to bring out the beast in him is Beth."

"Mackie Smith, I do believe you've lost your mind."

"Like I said, it just happened. We were both shopping at Book Emporium and he came over to speak with me. And it sort of went from there…but the more I'm around him, the more I really do like him."

Taurika shook her head while fanning herself dramatically. "Mackie, part of me is glad you've finally found some guy you admit liking. Another part can't help but worry about you. This will cause major tongue wagging around the office."

"I know. I've already thought about that. I've always been so protective of my image as an attorney and this could tar it good."

"Not permanently. Cheer up. You'll have your fifteen minutes of fame with the rumormongers and then they'll go on to someone else. But if you really care for Gordon, you can't run your life based on what people will think or say. I just hope you know what you're doing. You two seem so ill suited. Are you positive you want to keep seeing him?''

Mackie gave a noncommittal shrug. If it had been any other man, she could have easily answered no, but with Gordon, the answer didn't come so easily. She could feel her insides churning. Taurika, while trying to be supportive, had only reinforced Mackie's feelings that she dared not fall for Gordon. Any more than she already had, that is.

Determining that her growing obsession with Gordon needed to be scaled back, Mackie decided to do something—not break it off exactly, but pull back a little. When he called Wednesday morning suggesting lunch, she knew she couldn't accept.

"I'm afraid it's a carton of yogurt for me today. I've got a brief due in a couple of hours."

"Then I'll let you get to work."

"Yeah, I'd better. The brief's not going to write itself. Bye."

Gordon called back late that afternoon. "Did you get the brief finished on schedule?"

"Finished and filed with the court."

"Great. Why don't you stop by on the way home then? We can have a drink to celebrate the day's accomplishments…I'll whip up a meal. Ashley's in bed by eight so that even leaves some time to watch TV or whisper sweet nothings."

"Sweet nothings? Doesn't seem your sort of discourse."

"Oh, I have lots of hidden talents. Demonstrations available on request. But in your case, no request is necessary."

Mackie's determination to slow things down began to falter. It's now or never, she told herself. I'm sinking fast. "The paperwork stacked up while I was working on the brief," she told Gordon. "I don't know when I'll be finished with it all. Maybe we could get together in a couple of days."

"Sure," Gordon answered, disappointment evident in his tone. "I'll check with you later in the week."

After ringing off, Mackie sat staring at her blank computer screen, misery oozing from every pore. She hated being this low. Why did doing the right thing feel so awful? So Gordon Galloway was riveting, so he stoked something in her inner core. Some things were just not meant to be.

When Harris phoned a few minutes later inviting her to dinner the next day, Mackie took it as an omen that she was on the correct course. Harris had been away at a medical convention and she hadn't seen him since their aborted date at the gallery.

"I've missed you," he said.

"I've missed you, too." Well, she had. Sort of. *Oh, Mackie, be honest. You haven't given Harris Nelson a moment's thought lately.* So she was going to remedy that. "Instead of going out, how about dinner at my place?"

"You're not volunteering to cook, are you?" Harris's voice was wary. He knew her all too well.

"Ordering in, of course."

"In that case, what time should I show up and shall I bring white wine or red?"

The bottle of Beaujolais lay empty and Mackie was lamenting the fact she'd committed the evening to Harris. The meal was fine, but nothing else was. She'd always thought him entertaining, charming, witty. And he still was, yet...

Searching for something to talk about and without disclosing names or confidential information, she mentioned Gordon and Ashley's situation.

"Tough," Harris said. "Having sole responsibility for a child like that." He clinked his wineglass against hers. "Aren't you glad rug rats have never been on our agenda?"

Harris had every right to think he knew what he was talking about. Mackie and the crowd she and Harris ran with had often congratulated themselves on being part of an adults-only world—free to come and go on a moment's notice, no kid arguments over who got to ride by the window, quiet dinners with wine and piano music at Gershwin's instead of milk and Happy Meals at McDonald's. Yet the declaration had begun to ring hollow of late.

"I don't believe I've stated unequivocally that I *never* want children," she said defensively, setting her wineglass on the coffee table.

"Are my ears playing a trick on me?" Harris said,

grabbing her by the shoulders and giving her his version of a good-natured shake. "Or are you humming a different tune?" He leaned back, eyeing her closely. "Don't tell me the old biological clock has begun to tick?"

Mackie made a face. "I hate people saying that." Especially since she'd been hearing it too often of late. First Gordon, now Harris.

"Uh-oh, I've struck a nerve. And here I've been thinking Mackie Smith was focused squarely on career."

"I was. I am. I didn't say I *wanted* a baby, either. It's just that—"

"Sounds to me like you may have met a guy who would make the perfect father. Is that it? Am I going to lose you, Mackie?"

She looked pointedly at her watch. This wasn't a discussion she wanted to get into with Harris. "I have an early day tomorrow. We really need to say goodnight."

Harris opened his mouth as if to object, then sighed and looked around for his parka. "All right, I'll let you get your beauty sleep." He eased his parka hood over his head. "See you," he said. "And I have the feeling I won't be saying that much longer." Kissing her on the cheek, he quickly exited through the front door.

An hour later Mackie lay in the bathtub, dissecting her conversation with Harris. How many times over the years had she insisted to her friends and family that children were not in her scheme of things? Now the declaration was rebounding on her. Was her position set because it was what she really and truly wanted—or because she'd determined she had no choice?

Actually, until the past few weeks, a life without children had been a de facto state of affairs. Mackie had grown up as the only child of only children, with no cousins, nieces or nephews in the family picture. Just once had the possibility of a baby been part of her life—and that possibility had ended sadly, along with her marriage. Being honest with herself, Mackie had to admit that the real contributing factor to her decision that she wasn't cut out to be a mother lay there. But she'd come to terms with the decision long ago. Or had fooled herself into believing she had.

Two days had passed and Gordon sat by the telephone agonizing over whether or not to call Mackie. He'd sensed the negative undercurrent in their last conversation and he wasn't up for another turndown. Did she really mean it when she said "a couple of days," or did she mean "never"?

It had been a long time since he'd pursued a woman but not so long that he couldn't read the signs that said one was interested. And he could have sworn the signs were there with Mackie, that in the time they'd spent together, she'd become as infatuated with him as he with her. So why was she avoiding him? And why did that possibility make him feel as if he'd taken a kick to the ribs?

Well, he was no quitter. He'd give it one more try

and if Mackie begged off again... Gordon didn't even want to consider that.

When the phone rang Friday night and Gordon invited her to visit the zoo with him and Ashley the next day, Mackie was apprehensive. Already skittish about dating him, now she was faced with a family outing and taking their relationship to another level. It was one thing to be with Gordon, quite another to do the family bit. Then again, it wouldn't be their first jaunt as a threesome. And she desperately wanted to see them both. What could one more time hurt?

"I'll drive over to your place," she said, accepting the invitation. "No reason for you coming out here to pick me up."

"It's beautiful weather for the end of February," Gordon said, unfastening Ashley from her car seat and transferring her to a stroller. "Look, the trees are starting to bud."

"Well, we have to have some compensation for the high humidity and triple-digit heat in midsummer."

"Don't remind me. Summer'll be here soon enough. Just the other day, I saw an ad for beach towels."

They entered through the zoo gates and ambled around, enjoying the animals and savoring being outside. Ashley was too young to appreciate the animals for the novel creatures they were, but she did know the monkeys and lions and elephants from her books and from watching television.

"Ash, tell Mackie what a lion says."

"Grrr," the baby responded.

"And a tiger?"

"Grrr," Ashley repeated.

"And a monkey?"

"Grrr."

Mackie laughed.

"Oh well, two out of three," Gordon said, laughing, too.

He felt more laid-back today than he had in weeks. The trauma over his ordeal with Beth was fading into the past and Mackie had agreed to see him again. Intuition told him she'd been reluctant to be with him for a while. Now that same intuition told him that her reluctance had gone.

She, too, seemed more at ease today, less guarded with him, more attentive to Ashley. Despite the rocky beginning when she'd had Ashley thrust in her care, Gordon was beginning to suspect Mackie would make a good mother. She'd retrieved a tiny tennis shoe and put it back on, dabbed some sunscreen on Ashley's nose and cheeks and bought a stuffed giraffe for her at the zoo's gift shop.

Gordon had to stifle a laugh when he went to get cold drinks and returned to find an older couple fawning over Ashley and Mackie. "What a darling child. And so lucky to have a mother who spends quality time with her," the woman was telling Mackie.

Mackie was nodding and accepting the commentary, not once suggesting that the child in the stroller next to her wasn't her own. And to inquiring eyes, it did look indeed like a mother and child. After all,

Mackie was feeding graham crackers to Ashley and cleaning crumbs off her grungy little face like a pro.

The way Ashley was reveling in the attention took Gordon aback. He knew Ash needed a woman in her life someday—he simply hadn't thought about how strong the need already was.

The lady spoke to him when he walked up. "You have a lovely family," she said. "You must be very proud."

Gordon flicked a glance at Mackie before responding, "Yes, very proud."

"Now all you need," the gray-haired man chimed in, "is a boy to complete the package."

Both Mackie and Gordon nodded and moved along.

"What did you think about being called Ash's mom?"

Mackie smoothed down the little girl's flyaway brown bangs. "Complimented. As anyone would be."

"Not exactly anyone," Gordon answered. "Beth, for instance, apparently considers motherhood as nothing more than a meal ticket." He shook his head. "Sorry. I promised myself there would be no mention of her today. Only happy talk. Tell me, do you think Ash would welcome a little brother?"

Is that a leading question? Mackie could already picture that little boy—a miniature version of the man beside her. She felt a twinge of envy for the woman who would give Gordon that son.

He touched her shoulder. "Ash's brother?"

"Maybe in a year or two," Mackie managed to answer. "She's still a baby herself now."

They discussed grabbing a meal out after the zoo, but Ashley was getting cranky, and Gordon didn't trust her to behave in a restaurant.

"I can fix dinner if you can stand more of my cooking," he told Mackie on the drive home. Ashley, weary of whining and fussing, had given up and was dozing quietly in her car seat.

"Are you kidding? I'd love it. My whole existence is based on takeout, fast food and TV dinners. I can usually get a meal at Mom's, but it's not always worth the price of admission. Too much motherly advice goes along with it."

"OK, I'll try to limit the amount of advice with the meal. What are you in the mood for?"

"Whatever you're fixing."

Gordon carried Ashley into the house and laid her down to continue her nap. It was still early yet, only three-thirty, so Gordon brewed a pot of coffee and set out a plate of grapes. "I'm thinking of making chicken fajitas—my specialty, in case you didn't know."

"Fajitas sound great. Need me to do anything?"

He stared into the refrigerator. "I'm out of flour tortillas and a couple of other ingredients. Do you mind staying here with Ash while I dart to the store?"

"What do I do if she wakes up?"

"She probably won't, but if she does, prop her in her high chair and give her some juice or banana slices till I get home."

"Well…" Mackie was thinking of her first—and only—experience alone with Ashley. She could imagine the toddler jumping up screaming the minute Gordon left the house.

"I'll have my cell phone with me just in case. OK?"

"OK. I can manage that." She couldn't wimp out over the possibility of a few minutes by herself with Ashley.

Mackie had just switched on the television and settled into an easy chair when she heard the child's stirrings coming through the baby monitor. She climbed the stairs to the nursery. "Hi there, little one. Your daddy's gone bye-bye but he'll be back in a few minutes. Are you ready to get up?"

Ashley reached her arms in the air and Mackie lifted her from her crib. Her acceptance by the toddler giving her more confidence, Mackie changed a diaper, then carried Ashley into the kitchen and settled her into the high chair. "Do you want a banana?"

Ashley answered with an exaggerated nod. "Mmm," she said as the banana slices were placed in front of her.

Grocery bag in hand, Gordon leaned against the doorjamb leading to the kitchen and watched the woman and child. Neither was aware of his presence.

"Say Mackie. Mack..ie."

"Maa."

"That's it. Mackie."

"Maa Maa."

Gordon could have sworn there was a look of pleasure on Mackie's face when Ashley's words came closer to ''Mama'' than ''Mackie.'' He tapped on the open door announcing his arrival.

''I think she's finished her snack,'' Mackie said, dampening a paper towel to clean off the smeared fruit.

Once that was done, Mackie sat on a bar stool, watching Gordon at the butcher block island, cutting up vegetables. Ashley was toddling around, a piece of bell pepper in one hand and in the other, a wheeled toy popcorn popper, which she pushed across the floor, giggling at the clatter it made.

''Need me to chop or stir?''

''Nah. Just make sure Ash doesn't sneak out one of the doors. She's figured out how to turn handles and I don't want her making a bid for freedom. In the meantime I'll open a bottle of wine. All great cooks cook with wine.''

''Wine in fajitas?''

''No, the wine goes in the cook. And in you, too, if you'd like a glass.''

As he uncorked a bottle of Orvieto, Mackie moved Ashley away from the refrigerator. Little fingers had mastered that door as well. ''No mustard for you,'' she told the toddler, taking the squeeze jar from her hand and placing it back in the refrigerator door shelf.

''You have to keep a constant vigil,'' Gordon said. ''Now that she's mobile she's into everything. The telephone's a favorite—I think she dialed Denmark last week. But there's also the fireplace ashes, the bookshelves, the television dials, the cat's litter box…'' He laughed.

And Beth is too harebrained to keep any kind of vigil. No wonder he'd panicked about her having visitation and being alone with Ashley. For the first time, Mackie truly understood the depth of Gordon's concerns about shared custody. Ashley was now roving from one kitchen cabinet to another, testing the security latches on each. She then ambled over to Gordon, wrapping little arms around his pants leg.

"Speaking of the cat, where is Cleo?" Mackie asked.

"Hiding behind the sofa," Gordon answered. "She's become a master at keeping a low profile when Ash is around." Just then a skillet and a saucepan clattered onto the floor. Ashley had turned loose of Gordon and opened the cabinet under the range top where the cookware was stored.

"Maybe it'd be better if I just hold you while Daddy cooks." Mackie picked up the baby and sat at the kitchen table with Ashley in her lap, entertaining the baby with the motions to "Itsy Bitsy Spider."

"You're full of surprises," Gordon said. "First the snowflake songs and now this. Where did you learn all those juvenile ditties?"

Mackie shrugged. The day had been pleasant and she and Gordon were definitely growing closer, but she wasn't yet ready to reveal that a book of nursery rhymes lay at the bottom of her dresser drawer. A book bought long ago, when her dreams—her hopes—had not been trodden upon.

CHAPTER EIGHT

DINNER was finished and Mackie was cleaning the kitchen while Gordon bathed Ashley and put her to bed. He'd invited Mackie to join in, but she'd begged off, saying it probably wasn't a good idea to interrupt Ashley's routine. She stood at the kitchen sink, scraping dishes for loading into the dishwasher and mulling over the dynamics between her and Ashley.

Why was it that all of the child's capers had become so cute and engaging? She felt like a doting aunt...maybe even a doting mother. Instead of extricating herself the way she'd determined she should, Mackie knew she was growing inexorably attached to the girl.

Mackie couldn't help wondering whether she found Ashley so appealing because of the baby herself or because she was Gordon's daughter. It was difficult to separate her feelings for the two. Then again, maybe it didn't matter. As Beth had so profitably discovered, they came as a set, not to be separated.

"Shall we finish off that wine?" Gordon suggested, returning to the kitchen. He reached for the bottle and refilled their glasses.

Glasses in hand, they went to the family room and

took seats on the couch, a cushion separating them. Gordon looked her way and rested an arm across the unoccupied space between them. "So did you enjoy this sampling of family life?" He inched closer, placing his hand on the shoulder of her black velour sweatshirt.

"Every single minute." She took a sip of wine, all too aware of his fingers caressing the fabric, then playing along the vertebrae in her neck. Each touch brought out a new tingle.

"This is nice," Gordon drawled.

"The sweatshirt?"

"Touching you." He took her glass from her hand and set it on the end table, then slipped an arm around her, bringing her nearer.

She closed her eyes as he planted kisses on her neck, her cheeks, the corners of her mouth, then fully on her parted lips. Her hand went up to graze his face, the combination of soft skin and bristly five-o'clock shadow pleasing to her fingers.

Either the wine or Gordon's kisses were having a definite effect on her and Mackie was pretty sure she knew which. As delightful as this moment was, it was time to put on the brakes. If she wasn't going to give up the relationship, at least she could slow it down. She and Gordon were survivors of bad marriages, scarred and battered by their experiences. Nothing could be dumber than leaping precipitously into some kind of dalliance or affair. When the kiss broke, she said, "This is a beautiful house."

"...Yes," he responded, nuzzling her neck.

But she pulled away. "I'm guessing it was your aunt's."

"OK," he said resignedly. "I get the message. Less lovemaking, more talk." He leaned back and entwined his hands behind his head. "Yes, it was Aunt Hildy's home for fifty years and the most personal part of her bequest…maybe that's why it's my favorite part. Ash and I lived in a rented duplex near the university and I couldn't resist moving in here. Since the romancing has been put on hold, shall I give you a tour?" There was no rancor in his tone.

At her nod, he rose and held out a hand to her.

Mackie had seen most of the downstairs, so that piece of the tour was nominal. Then he motioned her up the staircase leading to the second floor. This was a large house, especially for two people, and there were numerous spare rooms that sat unoccupied or served as storage for boxes and extra furniture.

"As you can see, there's much to be done yet."

Mackie could just envision the possibilities: his and her studies, a game room, children's rooms. At present there were only the nursery and master bedroom being used on that level. She could envision the possibilities for that master bedroom, too. The feel of Gordon's touch was still on her skin, the memory of his kiss too recent in her mind. She moved on down the hall. His bedroom was dangerous territory.

"And what do we have here?" Mackie gestured to the surplus filling the next area she saw. Not just furniture, but knickknacks, books and old maga-zines, files.

"Aunt Hildy had so much. You should see the attic. I'm still culling out stuff," he explained. "Go-ing to give most of it away, but the hardest part is deciding what to keep."

"Quite a chore."

"Yeah, but by poring through all her things, I feel like I'm finally getting to know my aunt."

Mackie looked at him aghast. "You didn't know her well and she left everything to you?"

"Uh-huh. It's a long story. If you'd like, I could make some decaf and tell you all about it."

"I do want to hear, but another time, I think. It's nearly midnight and I don't want to overstay my welcome."

"No danger of that," he said, as they made their way down the stairs.

At the front door, Mackie knew he was going to kiss her again and he did. Those soft lips, that teas-ing tongue. It felt so perfect being in his arms.

How could she desire him so much and yet have so many qualms about their future? Was it a female trait to question every move in the game of love the way she was doing? Surely not. Such indecision would bring life to a standstill. It was just her. Mackie wished she could be the love 'em and leave 'em type, but she wasn't. And right now she was in a purgatory of her own making.

Twelve hours had passed but Mackie could still re-capture Gordon's kiss. All she had to do was close her eyes and she was back there in his arms, Gordon pressing her against his body, his scent a betwitching combination of citrusy men's cologne and sweet baby lotion. Perhaps not the most romantic formula but sufficient to make her light-headed just at the thought. She wasn't ready to feel this way.

And Ashley wasn't alleviating this emotional morass, either. All along Mackie had considered her a barrier to any permanent partnership with Gordon, but her sentiments had softened toward the little girl. And now a bond existed that she couldn't deny. What was it—other than Gordon—that drew her to this child? Did she need proof that all those awful accusations of her ex-husband...?

Mackie had believed she was rid of the effects of Bruce's maltreatment. But perhaps she wasn't. Eight years had passed and she'd had no serious relationship in all that time. Now all that was different. Mackie knew her feelings for Gordon were no fly-by-night emotions that would vanish when the new wore off. Yet Bruce's hateful words kept cropping up, making her question herself, keeping her from living life to the fullest.

Her confusion escalated when Gordon phoned in the afternoon. "I've got a busy week coming up—midterm exams—but if you're free, I thought we might have dinner Thursday."

Mackie could hear Ashley jabbering in the background and wasn't certain whether dinner meant another cook-in at his house or a night on the town.

Mackie didn't know which would be better...
whether she needed more time with Gordon alone to
continue getting to know the man...or conversely
whether repeated exposure to Ashley would take the
bloom off the rose and end all the soul-searching.

All Mackie knew was that she couldn't refuse
him. No matter if he chose to cook, dine out, or rip
open bags of corn chips and cans of Pepsi and call
it a meal, she wanted to be with him again. Her only
lament was that Thursday seemed eons away. "I'm
free," she said.

"Great, Ashley's nanny has agreed to stay over.
Seven-thirty OK?"

Gordon hung up, rescued the cat from Ashley's
grip on its ears, then leaned back against the kitchen
counter. As many times as his head said that Mackie
Smith wasn't the right type of woman for him, his
heart didn't care anymore. And in spite of her in-
experience with children, Mackie was making a real
effort with Ashley. The two were getting along fa-
mously.

He could still see them giggling hysterically as
Mackie bounced Ashley horseylike on her leg yesterday, Mackie's laughter as infectious as Ash's. So
where was it written that he shouldn't be going out
with Mackie? Contrary to his earlier opinions, she
was no witch on a broom. The woman he was getting
to know was...likable...pleasant to have around...
special. Very very special.

                    *   *   *

Lightning zigzagged over the western horizon when Gordon picked Mackie up at her town house. By the time they arrived at Café Madrid, it had begun raining hard. He wrapped one hand around her waist, and held an umbrella aloft with the other as they maneuvered through puddles on a mad dash into the restaurant.

"A night like this calls for wine," Gordon decreed. So they ordered a bottle of Spanish Rioja and an assortment of tapas and sat at a table by the window, listening to the rumbling thunder and watching the rain trickle down the glass.

At first the conversation was routine, talk of his day and her day, but mellowed by the wine, Gordon ventured, "Tell me more about your marriage."

"And spoil a lovely evening? No way."

"It'd help me know you better." He took her hand, turning it in his to trace the lines in her palm. "I see a woman afraid to reveal her past," he said, mimicking the fortune-teller. "The lines show that the lady will have great happiness if she opens her heart to her companion."

"Do the lines also mention whether the lady will win the lottery Saturday?"

"Nothing so frivolous. Only matters of the heart."

Nervously Mackie toyed with her earring, wondering what she could say to curb his interest in this particular segment of her life. "The divorce was a long time ago—over eight years now," she finally managed. "Ancient history."

"I like history, remember?" He wasn't going to be put off.

"OK, you asked for it... I was in my second year of college and Bruce was already working on his master's in business when we met at a campus party." Her fingers went back to the earring. "Surely you don't want all the grim details about what went awry, do you?"

"Why not? You're privy to the worst of *my* marital woes." He sandwiched her hand between the two of his.

Mackie had confided in few people about the way Bruce had belittled her, tromped on her self-image with both feet. There was no way Gordon would find the human doormat she'd been back then appealing. "Oh, just the usual bad marriage scene." She pulled the hand away and wrapped it around the bulb of her wineglass.

"I think there's more to it than that. And I don't want you to hold back. I want to know everything."

The way he looked at her, as if he could see into her soul, brought words to the surface, words Mackie thought she'd never speak.

"It started soon after the wedding," she began. "Put-downs, insults, criticism. This from the man who'd told me how wonderful—how perfect—I was when he asked me to marry him. Now, there was nothing right with me. According to Bruce I was fat, my hair was mousy, my wardrobe dowdy. Nothing I did to improve myself seemed to make a difference.

"He even persuaded me to give up college for a

job. Although my grades were good, he kept predicting that wouldn't last when I got to the tougher higher level courses. And he was continually suggesting that I'd be wasting my time on a degree because I wasn't destined to go far up the career ladder. After all, I was an imbecile—his word... I couldn't even master the simple rudiments of 'women's work,' couldn't cook, couldn't sew...''

She hesitated. "Well, you get the picture."

"Yeah, and it's not a pretty one. Sounds like a real bully. Did he ever hit you?"

"Never. There was no physical abuse. I'd have run out the door with the first slap. It took me a while to realize that emotional abuse could be just as damaging."

"Going back to college and then choosing law school showed a lot of courage."

"It wasn't easy. My ego had taken a battering. But eventually I started regaining my confidence and realizing that I had the potential after all."

"And the interest in family law came out of your own experience?"

She nodded. "I wanted to help women who were in the same fix I'd been in."

"So are you totally soured on marriage?"

"No, I'm just waiting for Tom Cruise to leave Nicole for me," she teased. Enough of heavy topics.

"Shucks," he answered, snapping his fingers. "Little hope for us mere mortals. But if you do have to settle for a guy who's not Tom Cruise, would you want kids?"

"I don't know." Until meeting Gordon and Ashley Mackie would have said, "probably not." But now... "The mommy track is tough—that double role is really difficult for a woman." That was a simpler explanation than telling him her ex-husband had convinced her she'd be a horrible mother. It was also the explanation she'd always given herself, the way she'd justified the life she led.

"It's easier, you know, if she's married to a man who carries his share of the load."

When Mackie didn't respond, Gordon went on, "So you don't see children in your future?" He watched her expectantly, afraid he knew what her answer would be.

Mackie paused, thoughtfully sipping her wine. "I suppose I haven't planned on that," she said honestly.

"Plans change."

"Frankly I'm not sure I'd make a very good mother," she confessed. "When I first married, I wanted a child...children." *Until circumstances— and Bruce—shot down that notion.* "Now I suppose I'm gun-shy." Although being with Ashley had begun to resurrect that desire. But could she do it? Could she be a good mother? Mackie questioned her abilities more than ever.

"Oh, I think Mackie Smith would be good at anything she put her mind to," Gordon said reassuringly. "Including mothering."

"You sound like my mom."

"It's the parent in me. Pops out without warning."

"You must be a natural father." Mackie was ready to redirect the focus of their conversation.

"Guess so. It sure *feels* natural. Even though Ashley wasn't a planned baby, I was euphoric when I heard she was on the way. I knew she would change my life. She has, that's for sure, in ways I could have never imagined. Without warning I was a single dad with a brand-new baby and a wife on the run."

"How did you manage?"

"The same way women do in the identical situation. I just did. Luckily I'd read a ton of baby-care books during the pregnancy. And I got lots of encouragement and practical advice from friends and family. Now I see that everything worked out for the best."

"So you're no longer mad at Beth for what she did?"

"For leaving, no. At least not anymore. For coming back—trying to take Ashley—yes. I'm not sure how long it'll take me to recover from the terror of that episode. Without that little girl, my life would be meaningless. But I'm trying to get past the anger. I know that's best for Ashley. And for me, as well. I certainly don't hold Beth's shenanigans against all women, whatever you may have thought."

Even with the hammering he'd taken from Beth, Gordon figured that eventually he would marry again, father more babies. Yet the future wife had always been amorphous. Now she was beginning to take shape in his mind. As he stared into her face, he knew he was falling for Mackie Smith. If only he could convince her that she'd be a good mother for Ashley.

"So how did the midterms go?" Mackie asked, varying the subject again, as though intuiting his thoughts.

"The usual. A couple of students tearing into class late because they'd pulled an all-nighter cram session, another complaining that the exam covered stuff never mentioned in any of my lectures, someone grousing that he thought the test was next week."

Gordon chuckled. "Every semester, it's the same, as if there's a script for the kids to follow. Now that spring break is upon us, I have to admit I'm as happy as the students to have a hiatus. Ashley and I expect to see a lot of you over the break." He drained the rest of the bottle into their wineglasses.

Mackie was pleased that they were at a stage for Gordon's feeling free to make claims on her time. And with the wine working its magic, her qualms temporarily faded into the background.

When Gordon dropped her off at her town house later that evening, Mackie invited him in. "I wish I could," he said. "But I need to rescue the nanny. Are you available for dinner tomorrow?"

Here we go again, she thought, the "I should decline" quandary. But the word "no" was quickly disappearing from her vocabulary when it came to Gordon. She could only say, "Yes."

"Great. I'll call you in the morning."

"Fine." She unlocked the door and leaned against the frame, wishing the evening weren't ending. Tomorrow seemed so far off.

Gordon propped a hand against the jamb and gazed into her eyes a moment, before bending to press his lips against hers. She'd been waiting for his kiss all evening and it didn't disappoint. First a gentle brush as one might kiss a baby. Then his hand moved from the doorjamb to claim her nape, and the baby kiss shifted into one of the genuine adult variety.

Mackie could smell the scent of cologne from his skin...could detect the taste of Spanish wine on his lips. Her eyes, even closed, could see the passion-glazed blue of his eyes. His lips moved over hers, heightening her senses, all of which seemed to be in play here. Her fingers moved beneath his jacket, delighting in the touch of male muscles beneath his starched cotton shirt. Her ears detected the heaviness of his breathing...and her own.

She wanted him to drag her inside and close the door behind them. She wanted more than that...for him to carry her upstairs to her bed à la Clark Gable in *Gone With the Wind*. Mackie could feel her body heat to a dangerous level. In another minute she'd be ripping Gordon's shirt off and carrying *him* up the stairs. Time to rein in her hormones before she ended up letting her libido rule her life. She forced herself to break the kiss.

"I wish I could stay," he whispered.

"I wish you could, too." *But it's better that you can't.*

On Friday it was still raining. A slow, steady downpour now, unaccompanied by the theatrical displays of thunder and lightning. "Sorry I can't ask you out for dinner and dancing," Gordon said as Mackie unfolded her umbrella in his foyer. "It'd be a great excuse to take you in my arms."

Mackie loved to dance and the idea of an evening in Gordon's arms was glorious to contemplate. She could picture herself snuggling into his embrace, her head resting against his chest listening to his heartbeat as they moved to the music. The closeness of their bodies leading to a kiss...

Over and over, Mackie's thoughts lingered on Gordon's kisses. She could hardly wait for more. OK, so her libido was temporarily winning out. She'd treat it like a bad habit, smoking...overeating...and vow to give up Gordon tomorrow. Or the day after that.

Ashley was strapped in her high chair, just finishing a meal of spaghetti. Her chubby face was smeared with sauce, her fingers busily squishing the remnant strings of spaghetti into a reddish mass of pasta. "Maf," she squealed when Mackie entered the kitchen.

"Maf better stay out of harm's way if she values

her clothes," Gordon said, laughing. "It's straight to the bath for you, Mistress Ashley." He lifted the baby from the high chair, holding her at arm's length. "Come join us while I scrub off all these layers of food," he said to Mackie.

"OK." She followed father and daughter up the stairs.

Mackie watched while Gordon soaped and rinsed—and Ashley splashed—then she held a towel for Gordon to lift the wriggling baby into. Ashley smelled so sweet. Mackie kissed her neck and the little girl chortled approvingly.

Clad in pajamas, cuddling her teddy bear, Ashley was laid into her baby bed. When Gordon kissed her and said good-night, Ashley responded with, "Nite," but when Gordon and Mackie began backing away from the crib, the toddler squealed, "Maf stay."

He looked to Mackie for confirmation and she nodded, and began patting the toddler and humming a lullaby. Gordon listened a moment, then hurried on downstairs, a smile on his face.

"This is nice," Mackie said. They were sitting at the boothed kitchen table looking out the window. Twinkling lights were strung in the backyard trees, illuminating the rainfall that was kicking up tiny waves in the blue-hued water of the swimming pool.

"Sometimes I feel like the luckiest man alive. I never thought I'd live like this," Gordon said, gesturing at the scene. "Experience this kind of luxury." He twirled the stem of his wineglass between his palms.

"And yet you barely knew your aunt. You were going to tell me how this came to be."

He shook his head in wonderment. "It's a story that I can't explain. And neither can anyone in my family. Hildy Cuthbert was married to my great-grandmother's younger brother. They were a very close couple with no children, and after he died some twenty-five years ago, she became more and more a recluse, contact with the rest of the family petering out.

"Then after her death, I discovered I was her heir. But her will gave no reason why. She was quite a philanthropist, made some big donations to colleges and universities during her lifetime. So maybe she liked my profession. But that's only a guess. She'll always be an enigma.

"College professors make a fair living, but suddenly I found myself with more money than I'd ever dreamed of. I'm not complaining, you understand, but money alters things." He gazed off into the light-studded grounds for a minute before meeting Mackie's eyes once more.

"And is a magnet for people you wish would stay out of your life?"

"Bingo. Like I told you before, I'm willing to bet we'd never have seen hide nor hair of Beth if she hadn't heard through the grapevine about the money." He took Mackie's hand. "But there was even a silver lining in that. If not for Beth, I might not have found you. Might not have realized who and what was missing in my life. In a way, for me, money did buy happiness.''

"The money doesn't matter to me, Gordon.'' Something he needed to understand.

''I didn't think it did.''

''A lot of men would. Especially after your experiences with hangers-on...and with Beth. You probably imagined she and I would try to bleed you dry.''

''At first maybe...not after I got to know you. But hey, I didn't mean for us to stray off into such negative talk,'' he said sternly. Then he smiled. ''Earlier I mentioned dancing with you. There's no reason we can't do it here. May I have the honor, Ms. Smith?'' He stood and held out his hand.

Gordon had waited all evening to feel his body against hers, to hold her in his arms without interruption. He sensed Mackie wanted the same thing. Fortunately he didn't have to set the mood. The compact disc player was already loaded, the music he'd selected renditions of the slow, body-touching songs from past eras, and perfect for dancing.

Candles had been burning before. Now he turned off the lights, turned up the music and pulled Mackie into his arms, hugging her close.

They moved to the tempo. ''You're a good dancer,'' she said, leaning her head back to gaze into his eyes.

It took every ounce of Gordon's resolve to keep from lowering his head, touching her lips with his.

But he held off, savoring the moment. Besides, the way he felt right now, there was no way he could stop with kisses.

"I just paid you a compliment, Mr. Galloway."

His mind snapped back to her words. "...oh, my dancing. Four years of lessons—age twelve through sixteen. My mother believed boys should be able to move on a dance floor as well as on a football field. Called it being 'well-rounded.' I hated the lessons at the time, thought they would ruin my life, but to-morrow I'd better call Mother and say thanks." He caressed Mackie's cheek with his own.

"Hmm," she said. "Tell your mother thanks for me, too."

The song ended and he bent her backward in a deep dip.

"Wow!" Mackie exclaimed, as he raised her up. "Fred Astaire reincarnated. I'll bet the girls were really impressed with you in high school. Not too many teenage guys know a dip from a do-si-do."

"Except there were no dips or do-si-dos at those adolescent dances. No fox-trots or waltzes, either. The music was strictly disco or rock. All my lessons gone to waste."

"Wasted? I don't think so." She lay her head on his shoulder, he tightened his hold and once more they moved as one.

That song ended. Another began. Then another. They were lost in a world of their own as their bod-ies swayed in tandem. Then the tempo picked up— a tango.

"I forgot I put that on. Want to give it a try?"

Mackie moved back into his arms. The erotic beat seemed to activate every single nerve ending. The tango had to be the world's most erotic dance. Her thighs were welded to Gordon's as he guided her through the intricate steps. Faces together, leg over leg. She wished she had a fan handy like those Argentinean señoritas—she definitely needed one the way her temperature was soaring. A few degrees higher and she might have to rush outside and fling herself into the pool before she burst into flame.

Or better yet, to forget dancing and fling herself into Gordon's bed. Gordon's smoky gaze indicated that he was thinking similar thoughts. But the moment was lost when they heard Ashley's cry.

CHAPTER NINE

THE RAIN had stopped, the day was warm and spring-like, when Mackie went outside her town house to retrieve the morning newspaper. When she came inside, the phone was ringing and she snatched the receiver up, certain—or at least hopeful—that Gordon was the caller. Her attempt at an alluring whispery "hello" came out more a frog's croak than a female voice.

This is ridiculous—you're reacting like a fourteen-year-old in the throes of her first crush. But her feelings for Gordon were no simple crush that would vanish with the next good-looking guy who came her way. She was falling in love with him and as magnificent as that felt, the awareness was also frightening. It challenged all her concepts of who she was, what she wanted. Mackie Smith, family practice lawyer and crusader. Solidly on the career path to partnership—possibly even a judgeship down the line. Her concepts hadn't allowed room for husband and family...for love.

"You OK?" he asked. "You sound funny."

"Yes, sorry. Not enough coffee yet." Well, she probably did need more caffeine. Something to jolt her from this dreamlike state.

"How's Ashley?" The baby had awakened with

an upset stomach the night before and Gordon and Mackie had spent an hour ministering to her before Mackie went home. Or more accurately, Gordon was the one who'd done the ministering. Mackie's contribution consisted mostly of wringing her hands and wondering how to help.

"She was asleep again about thirty minutes after you left. From all signs, she's fully recovered from whatever bug was bothering her. Right now, she's giving Cleo a fit."

"Poor Cleo," Mackie said, laughing.

"Do you have plans for today? If not, spend it with us. Ash and I have decided a trip to the park is in order. Going to take advantage of the warm weather we're having."

Mackie hesitated. Despite the giant leap forward her relationship with Gordon had taken, that didn't mean his feelings matched hers. So he'd held her tight while they danced... Lots of men held their partners snugly. Conclusions of love certainly couldn't be drawn from that. So his good-night kisses made her toes curl—what about *his* toes?

Besides, there was Ashley to consider. Even if Gordon's feelings were deepening, he and his daughter were a package deal. Mackie still wasn't confident that she was ready to cope with that or that she'd be doing right by the child. Last night, she'd been so frightened and inept when Ashley was ill. Gordon knew exactly what to do to soothe her. But all Mackie could contribute was fetching cool washcloths and muttering inanities about everything being OK.

Surely some inborn mothering knowledge should have kicked in, told her what to do, how to doctor a sick child, but it hadn't.

"Sorry, not this time," she told Gordon. "My mother's invited me for lunch and shopping." *And would be delirious if I told her I needed to back out because I had a date with the two of you.* But Mom was a good excuse. And provided an opportunity for her to get her head on straight. Being with Gordon the past two nights had definitely destroyed any practical thinking.

"OK, if I can't talk you into today, how about tomorrow. The weather's supposed to be great—we could heat up the pool and take a dip, grill some hamburgers."

Mackie hesitated once more. Gordon would never understand her refusing two invitations in a row. Not anymore. If she said no now, he might not call again. Ambivalence aside, she couldn't bear for that to happen. Besides, she *wanted* to be with him. And if she was ever to stop this seesawing about Ashley, she needed more exposure to the little girl. "I'd like that. When do you want me there?"

Now. I want you here now. It had taken every ounce of Gordon's willpower to let her go last night. If Ash hadn't been ill, he simply wouldn't have. He wanted Mackie in his arms, in his bed…in his life. Permanently. He'd heard all the warning bells— you've only known her a short time…she's a career woman instead of the homebody you thought you needed…children haven't been on her agenda…you haven't dated anyone else since your divorce...you ought to play the field awhile and not propose to the first woman to cross your path.

None of the alarms drowned out the joy he felt when Mackie was around. It was becoming as impossible for him to imagine a life without her as to think of one without Ashley.

"I said when do you want me there? Is it that difficult a decision?" Mackie said teasingly. "Or are you thinking of reneging on the invitation?"

"Oh, no, just bemoaning the number of hours until you arrive. What do you say three on Sunday?"

"Three o'clock it is."

Mackie attended church services, detoured home to change into casual clothes, then on the way to Gordon's, stopped by Preston-Royal to shop. She'd only set out to find Ashley a new swimsuit, but spotted two adorable dresses in the children's store window, which she couldn't resist.

Deciding that Ashley was too young to be impressed with a gift of clothes, she crossed to another store a few doors down. There she bought an assortment of pool toys.

"Just a couple of things for Ashley," she said sheepishly, shifting the packages in her arms as Gordon met her at his front door, Ashley standing next to him, her arms squeezing the leg of his pants.

"A couple?"

"OK, three...four. I know I went overboard, but it

was fun. Once I got started, I couldn't seem to stop…hope you don't mind—''

"I don't mind at all," Gordon interrupted, pleased at Mackie's growing interest in his daughter. "Although Ash is going to wonder if Christmas has rolled around again.'' He picked up the little girl.

Surely this was a good sign, he thought. Mackie might have brought a single gift for Ashley and he wouldn't have read any special meaning into it. This treasure trove of presents, however, seemed to imply something more.

"Well, I wasn't here to celebrate Christmas with her, so I'm just making up for lost time,'' Mackie said, as they walked into the family room.

Gordon placed Ashley on the couch and Mackie handed her the shopping bags.

"Oooh.'' The baby lifted a pink ruffled dress with matching bloomers from the bag.

"We girls have to keep our wardrobes up,'' Mackie told her. "What do you think of this one?'' The second dress was pale yellow with smocking in front.

"Blue," Ashley gurgled.

"Uh-uh, yellow. Can you say yellow?''

"Fim,'' Ashley replied instead, discovering the swimsuit and the pool toys.

"Sure, we'll swim.'' Gordon looked Mackie's way. "Did you bring your suit along too?''

For the next hour, the three of them splashed in the pool. Eventually Ashley grew bored of the water play and struggled to get out. Gordon and Mackie stayed in the pool while the little girl toddled around the yard, chasing a ball.

"How long has she been walking?" Mackie asked, leaning her arms over the edge of the pool to watch Ashley.

"Almost six months now. She started early." From behind he wrapped his arms around Mackie, innocently resting his palms on the concrete deck. His bare chest immediately warmed her wet back; his touch and the closeness causing internal warmth and X-rated thoughts. He snuggled closer, dropping his hands from the deck to wrap them around her waist. Wandering fingers moved higher, scouting the border of her swim top.

"She'll see us," Mackie warned, her voice quivery, as Gordon brushed his lips across her neck.

"Ash isn't a skilled observer of such things. Not that she's had a lot of opportunity." He continued to rub his bare chest against her back. "Actually no opportunity at all. And I'm sure she's more interested in the ball than in my making love to you."

Was this what parents did? Steal embraces when the children weren't looking? The thought was provocative.

When Ashley tripped and fell flat, she squealed and came racing toward Gordon for a hug.

"Just when things were getting interesting," Gordon complained, tracing a finger along Mackie's earlobe before pulling himself out of the pool.

It was all Mackie could do to dog-paddle toward the ladder and pull herself out as well.